Madness Has a Moment and Then Vanishes Before Returning Again

Madness Has a Moment and Then Vanishes Before Returning Again

Benjamin DeVos

Dostoyevsky Wannabe

First Published in 2016
By Dostoyevsky Wannabe
All rights reserved
© 2016 Benjamin DeVos
All rights reserved.
ISBN-13: 978-1534681798
ISBN-10: 1534681795

Contents

"Be silent and listen: have you recognized your madness and do you admit it? Have you noticed that all your foundations are completely mired in madness? Do you not want to recognize your madness and welcome it in a friendly manner? You wanted to accept everything. So accept madness too. Let the light of your madness shine, and it will suddenly dawn on you. Madness is not to be despised and not to be feared, but instead you should give it life. If you want to find paths, you should also not spurn madness, since it makes up such a great part of your nature. Be glad that you can recognize it, for you will thus avoid becoming its victim. Madness is a special form of the spirit and clings to all teachings and philosophies, but even more to daily life, since life itself is full of craziness and at bottom utterly illogical. Man strives toward reason only so that he can make rules for himself. Life itself has no rules. That is its mystery and its unknown law. What you call knowledge is an attempt to impose something comprehensible on life."

— C.G. Jung

Inherently Naïve Optimism Complicates My Life

I was a rookie detective investigating my first homicide. I knocked on the suspect's door, and Ryan Gosling answered, wearing a bloodstained bowling shirt. I did not notice the blood at first. I was too distracted by his beautiful blue eyes. He was the perfect specimen of a man. He looked like the kind of man who could nurse a dying puppy back to health. I told him that I was investigating his eyes. Then I said that I was investigating a murder, which occurred the evening before at Lucky Strike Bowling Alley.

Ryan Gosling stated that he knew nothing about it. I said, "Your beautiful hair was at the crime scene." Ryan Gosling replied, "I am not sure how my hair could have fallen into someone else's possession." I told him that the victim's name was Jared Leto. Ryan Gosling said that he knew Jared Leto. The two of them had an ongoing rivalry as the two best bowlers at Lucky Strike. Then Ryan Gosling said, "Jared Leto got what was coming to him." I asked him for his alibi. Ryan Gosling told me that he was a part-time butcher and that he had spent the night before slicing bacon at his deli.

Without any hard evidence, I said that he was not under arrest. Then I asked him for a hug. He was hesitant, but I made it clear that it was purely platonic. Some of the blood from his bowling shirt got on my uniform, but I did not notice until I got back to the station. I was in a fantasy where Ryan Gosling and I were the two best friends that anybody ever had. The forensics team ran a DNA strand test on the sample, and the results came back that the blood indeed belonged to Jared Leto. I was so happy to have an excuse for returning to Ryan Gosling's house, even if it was to place him under arrest.

I was nervous when there was no answer at the front door, and I thought maybe he had skipped town. I decided to break in through the window. There was no sign of him on the first floor, but I could hear a metallic rasp coming from the basement. I followed the sound until I found Ryan Gosling, standing over a meat grinder, holding Jake Gyllenhaal upside down by his ankles. Jake Gyllenhaal's lower body was in a gory mound on the ground. I initially considered calling the paramedics, who I thought might have been able to separate the grinder from its housing so that the leftovers of Jake Gyllenhaal could remain, maybe in a museum, where future generations could behold the once promising young thespian.

Then I looked into Ryan Gosling's eyes. He was still very much alive, and still very much baby blue. "It's all over now," he said, slowly walking toward me with his arms wide open in anticipation of my embrace. I figured that there was no use ruining any more lives than necessary, and wrapped my arms around Ryan Gosling. For that moment he held me. I mean really held me. Then Ryan Gosling reached for a hammer on the shelf behind him and knocked me out with the pointy end.

Exercising Undue Influence Through Mental Distortion and Emotional Exploitation

As a group of paramedics entered the basement, I pretended to be asleep. My spine aligned along the concrete floor as they delicately pressed my chest to keep my ribs from breaking. They pressed until I coughed, just soft enough that it could be presumed a postmortem response. Then the paramedics pushed with enough force that the pressure seemed to run from my sternum through my skull, forcing my eyes open for the first time in several hours, which caused me to blink repeatedly as my retinas adjusted to the spotlight shining down on my face.

I noticed several FBI agents standing behind the paramedics. Gillian Anderson and David Duchovny were the lead investigators. They both stared at me with nondescript expressions that said, "I have seen this type of thing before. This is nothing new." By that point, I realized that there were going to be a lot of questions, and I needed to come up with an excuse for being in that basement. I told them that I could not remember anything because the impact of the concrete against my head had scrambled my memory. Gillian Anderson said that I had experienced traumatic brain injury, also known as amnesia.

David Duchovny told me to quit bullshitting, then left the room for approximately five to ten minutes before returning with the most beautiful photograph that I had ever seen. "Looks familiar, does it not?" asked David Duchovny. I said, "No." Then I said, "That is the ugliest man I have ever seen." David Duchovny looked at Gillian Anderson, at the photograph, then back at me. "Are you prepared to repeat that statement while hooked up to a polygraph machine?" I agreed, and after approximately fifteen to twenty more minutes had completed their test.

Gillian Anderson told me that according to my skin conductivity, I indeed believed that the person in the picture, the presumed suspect, was indeed the ugliest man I had ever seen. She told me that I could go home, and after reminding me exactly where I lived, decided that it would be better for her to drive me there. David Duchovny felt bad about doubting my post-traumatic condition and volunteered to take me instead, which was agreed upon after I told Gillian Anderson that I forgave David Duchovny, and wanted to talk about guy stuff.

On the way back to my house I asked David Duchovny if he would be willing to stop by a dark alley across town where I could buy some painkillers from a drug dealer because my headache was killing me. He told me that it was highly irregular, but after repeatedly asking him whether or not he remembered back at the station when he cursed at me and called me a liar, he eventually agreed to help me buy drugs. When we arrived at the dark alley, I got out of the car and pretended to feel very dizzy. After collapsing onto the ground, David Duchovny rushed out of the vehicle and asked, "Are you alright?"

Those were his last words before being knocked out cold, blindsided by a beaming Ryan Gosling. "Is he handsome enough for you?" I asked, looking into his beautiful blue eyes. "He will do just fine," replied Ryan Gosling. Then we loaded David Duchovny's unconscious body back into the car and drove to Ryan Gosling's house before anyone could spot us.

Accelerating Toward the Next Stage of Life

Ryan Gosling was taking an extraordinarily long time deciding how he wanted to dispose of David Duchovny. Since the police had taken the meat grinder as evidence, he was trying to come up with something more creative. He looked around the basement uninspired. I suggested that we hurry because Gillian Anderson would probably be breaking down the door at any moment in search of her missing partner. Ryan Gosling told me that I, as the inferiorly handsome man, should keep my comments to myself unless I was speaking with the specific purpose of complimenting his good looks.

I started to feel as if the entire situation was an opposing factor to my integrity, sanity, and sobriety. I hoped that one day I would be able to look back on my time with Ryan Gosling and laugh. There was no going back because presumably David Duchovny would not forgive me for leading him into the den of a murderer. My best option, I decided, was to plead temporary insanity, attributed it to the hammer's impact on my brain. In the meantime, I slowly moved toward the shelf where Ryan Gosling got the hammer.

Beneath the shelf was a chainsaw, which, before I became lucid, had suggested we use to chop up David Duchovny into little pieces. Ryan Gosling rejected my suggestion, calling it, "Cliché amateur bullshit." I picked up the chainsaw and tried to rev the engine. Ryan Gosling laughed and said, "There's no gas in it, stupid." He pulled the hammer out of his tool belt, and, with a deranged look on his face, charged toward me. I swung the chainsaw in self-defense, and inadvertently sliced open Ryan Goslings jugular with the teeth of the blade. Blood squirted everywhere. David Duchovny cheered, "Hooray! You got him." I caught Ryan Gosling as he fell, and pinched shut the severed artery by reaching my hand into his neck. David Duchovny told me to "Let the bastard bleed out," but I was a vegan. I valued all life.

I called the paramedics, who took Ryan Gosling to the hospital where he got three hundred stitches across his neck. The traumatic incident led Ryan Gosling down a spiral of nightmares and chronic depression. He tried to kill himself in prison but was saved by one of the guards. Eventually, he was able to cope with his demons through intense psychotherapy and The Power of Now by Eckhart Tolle, which he read over and over again on a never-ending cycle.

David Duchovny made it out of the basement unscathed, and while he did not arrest me due to my foolproof temporary insanity defense, I did have to turn in my badge and resign from law enforcement forever, which I was more than happy to do. I was experiencing insomnia ever since the incident of accidentally almost murdering Ryan Gosling, the man I most admired in the world for his handsomeness when really he was just another egomaniac set on slaughtering innocents. Self-centeredness was my biggest pet peeve, which was the real reason my perception of Ryan Gosling shifted from a prepossessing obsession to loathing.

The Flexible Nexus Between Past, Present, and Future

Paul Rudd noticed a subtle melancholy that was just slightly detectable beneath my asymmetrical haircut and offered to take me out for the evening. He said that Rush was in town for their fortieth anniversary tour and that if I wanted, we could eat some food, then go to the show. I told him that was a solid plan, and that Rush was a perfect choice of music for an introspective, sad person like myself because of their upbeat tempo and lyrics that drew heavily on science fiction, fantasy, history, and philosophy.

Paul Rudd and I decided that tacos would be a good food to eat before Rush because of their spice and complimentary flavor to the pitcher of house margaritas we were drinking. I was more into drugs, and Paul Rudd was more into drinking. I said, "I wish we had some weed," and Paul Rudd said, "Check this out," and pulled a glowing bag of gold cap mushrooms from his pocket. I told him a recent study showed that mushroom trips could help victims of post-traumatic stress disorder, of which I was one, and Paul Rudd replied, "I read that review on the Internet too! That is why I bought these. Small world."

I thought about how big the world was as I ate mushrooms on the way to the concert venue, laid all the way back in my seat as Paul Rudd played air bass in silence. In line at will call, Paul Rudd surprised me again with two fat joints, which he asked if I would put in my shoe since I was the only one of us wearing socks. Once inside, I transitioned into a not unpleasant intoxicated-like state, followed by an all-consuming sense of purpose to study each and every person around me for his and her behavioral traits and characteristics. In a trancelike condition, with one eye closed (one spotlight from the stage was shining directly onto the left side of my face), I watched an endless outpouring of anticipatory conversation, bizarre figures, and demonstrative, sometimes passionate exchanges, and with my shut eye envisioned the world ripe with pastoral imagery.

I felt very interested in the real-life connections between living beings. Paul Rudd could not stop smiling, and seemed to speak in the voice of a leprechaun for the rest of the night, which I thought was pleasant. When Rush came out onto the stage, the crowd exploded in a sight so bursting and full of color that the world seems hardly able to contain it. I was momentarily anxious, as my heart was beating much faster than usual, or so it felt, but Paul Rudd mellowed me out by reminding me about the joints in my shoe, which we proceeded to smoke.

As I looked around, everyone in the crowd was smoking reefer, and a big cloud of smoke was slowly forming overhead. For a moment, I forgot that we were indoors, and asked Paul Rudd if he by chance had an umbrella in case it started to rain. Paul Read shouted, "We are inside!" over the music.

About halfway through the show, I needed to pee due to the excessive margarita consumption during dinner. Paul Rudd and I wiggled out of the crowd, saying, "Excuse me," nearly one hundred times before we were in the clear. It was quite freeing, and I reached a sublime level of fearlessness and ambition. The expanse felt transcendent. Once in the bathroom, I felt totally reborn as my bladder emptied, releasing me from the burden that had reduced my maximum fun capacity, which after peeing was sky high. In my enthusiastic state, I was able to convince Paul Rudd to leave the show early to get waffles for a late night snack.

The maple syrup gave me a sugar rush, which spurred my imagination to generate a utopian world where only the most spectacular moments existed. It was a natural extension of the universe, carefully maintained, and an idealistic revelation of what human beings at their best were capable of—a society where love was the transmogrifying construct that abolished antipathy. That's when Paul Rudd, who was in a zoned-out trance-state, depressively interrupted my vision with a maelstrom of stammering. He was remembering something tragic that was shifting his gears into a dangerous place, and it was up to me to help him.

I said, "I am here for you. Everything will be okay." Paul Rudd's eyes came into focus, and he said, "For a second I felt like I had forgotten who I was. My entire life was a blank slate. I was nobody." I told him, "You are somebody. That is why you are here." Once I felt Paul Rudd had regained his calm, we finished eating our waffles in silence, each of us reflecting on where we were going, and where we had been, trying to stay upbeat as the world continued to spin.

"Follow your inner moonlight; don't hide the madness."

— Allen Ginsberg

I Want to Believe

Two months ago I was sitting in the backyard when I witnessed a stunning explosion in the forest outside my house. A green light filled the atmosphere, and there was a commotion like a thousand spirits screaming in the night. I will never forget how the asteroid sounded during the collision. It sounded like a fist punching through the Earth. I rose from my hammock and hazarded into the forest to see if I could determine where the asteroid laid its impact. It was not that hard to find. I only had to go in the reverse direction of the animals that were running out of the forest, wailing, howling, barking, and tweeting in a cloud of terror.

I forged ahead, upstream through a river of frightened fur, until at last I arrived at the smoldering spot in the forest where a crater the size of a Buick lay. The smell of that smoke was unlike anything I'd experienced in my entire life. It was the smell of a goblin's breath hot on your back as he chases you through a warm sewage system. In the middle of the crater, there was an egg, the color of an almond. I ventured further into the impact zone, though I knew that I should have called a scientist instead. It was as if that egg had a hypnotic hold on my psyche and I couldn't help but walk toward it.

The very top of the egg looked like the protuberance of a baboon's buttocks, fleshy and round. What happened next changed me forever.

The egg split open, and out of it emerged an alien, who would one day be known as Lady Gaga. She looked as if she had a high-temperature fever at full throttle. Her eyes were popping out of their sockets, slowly receding into her head as a green ooze poured from her mouth like radioactive saliva. Her face had an excruciatingly neutral expression. She didn't speak any Earthly language, but when she did make noises, her voice resonated in a mezzo-soprano range that left me speechless.

Lady Gaga could convey an array of emotions without speaking. For example, I knew she was sad and hungry when she lay supine in the dirt, eating ferns with hot green tears dripping from the whites of her eyes. She slowly crept away, and I followed her until we reached a ranch on the outskirts of the forest. She appeared happy when a cow approached and proceeded to tear it apart with her long nails and teeth like a human blender. Her roar of victory was deafening.

She made a dress to wear out of the raw beef and continued on her journey. I couldn't hear anything after that, but it seemed like Lady Gaga was singing by the way her mouth moved incessantly and her throat vibrated like there was a pure wave massager in her torso. It was hard to tell if she was a monster, or if she was just born that way. In any case, I was frightened for my life.

I continued to follow her until she reached an underground cave beneath a highway overpass. Lady Gaga's glowing body lit the cavern. I tried to keep up, though my eyesight was continuously straining and deteriorating as we walked. It got to the point where I could not breathe due to the brutally suffocating smell coming from inside of the cave, so I idly tried to find my way out with most of my senses in jeopardy. All I had left was touch, and with each time I felt the wall, it seemed like my body grew more and more numb, until I couldn't feel anything at all. I was anesthetized on the outside and filled with regret on the inside for following Lady Gaga without thinking about the possible consequences. Then everything went black, and not even my thoughts could penetrate the obscurity.

When I woke up, I was in my backyard as if I'd never left. I thought maybe it was a dream, but then remembered the smells, the sensations, and knew that what I'd seen was real. I couldn't explain it, what Lady Gaga was. She was a species that neither the world nor I seemed ready to accept. I wanted to tell everyone what I'd seen, but I knew nobody would believe me. So I kept it to myself, watching and waiting for more like her to emerge from the forest. But no more aliens appeared. None like her anyway.

Extreme States of Being Are a Unique Kind of Blessing

I was walking through the woods when I heard something snap. That something was my leg being broken by a bear trap. A scruffy man with a hatchet approached from the clearing. I hoped he was a kind lumberjack, and not an axe murderer. His name was Joaquin Phoenix. He asked what I was doing in his forest, and said, "There is no hunting without permission." I told him that I was just taking in the fresh air, not hunting. Then I announced that I was in tremendous pain, and needed a doctor as soon as possible.

Joaquin Phoenix squinted as if he were trying to see me from very far away. I heard a growling sound, which at first I thought was Joaquin Phoenix's stomach. Despite having cultivated a dense beard, he was pale and appeared malnourished. I realized that the sound was actually a bear, emerging from the thicket before sliding to a halt in front of Joaquin Phoenix.

A spray of forest floor struck me in the face. The ginormous bear rumbled and roared. Joaquin Phoenix fell to the dirt and played dead as the bear crept forward until it was hovering over his body, snarling ferociously. I tried to find a cell phone signal, but we were too far from civilization.

The ginormous bear swatted its paw, and with one swipe, tossed Joaquin Phoenix into the air. Joaquin Phoenix did a three-sixty before landing and going limp. He did not move even as the bear's nose nudged his head and sniffed his hair. My eyes ached from staying open for so long. I blinked and tried to take a step back. When I did, I screamed in pain from the bear trap's hold on my bloody thigh.

The bear turned toward me, and with a loud roar, reared on its massive haunches. The bear knocked me down and pinned me to the ground, preparing to maul me with its giant haunches. The bear growled a foot away from my face, spit and hatred spraying from its lips. Then I heard the sound of another snap as Joaquin Phoenix plunged his hatchet through my leg, freeing me from the trap originally meant for the bear.

My howls of agony were so loud, so violent, that the bear fled frightened back through the forest. Joaquin Phoenix chased after it, brandishing his hatchet and shouting obscenities. It seemed that he had channeled his inner huntsman. I crept silently through the underbrush, blood oozing from the stump where my shin used to be. The sun went down, and I waited in hopes that Joaquin Phoenix would return to me with a doctor, and not a new taste for killing.

I had nothing to use for protection. All I could do was wait and bleed, trying to ignore the warm trickle running up my thigh. I ate some mushrooms that were growing at the base of a tree and began to hallucinate another bear, even bigger and meaner than the first. In my psychedelic state of dread, I was able to muster enough energy to hop and gradually made my way back out of the woods, to the car I had parked by the side of the road. The big mean bear rocked my car back and forth as I turned the key in the ignition. I only then realized that the leg, which I usually used to drive was the one that had gone missing.

All I could do was idle in agony, but this time the blood trickle ran cold. Fear slowly overwhelmed me as I repeated, "This will all be over soon." That was when Joaquin Phoenix, who heard my cries of terror, and the revving of my engine, broke the passenger side window with his hatchet and said: "I will drive you to the hospital, now."

Madness Has a Moment and Then Vanishes Before Returning Again

It was the first full moon of the year when Bradley Cooper pinned me to a bench in the park and asked, "Are you going to protect me from the werewolves?" I smiled and blushed a little. Then the bushes rustled. The sound kept getting louder and louder and louder until suddenly a big ass werewolf appeared. I pulled Bradley Cooper behind me, which only made the werewolf angry. It jumped approximately ten feet over my head, and then with a howl, started smashing Bradley Cooper against the ground like a ragdoll.

A bloodied Bradley Cooper told me to make a run for it, and that he would catch up. "A run for what?" I asked. "Just go!" he said. "I am done for."

"Really?" I thought. "Is he just going to give up?" I decided to follow the big ass werewolf back to its cave, and when I figured it was gone, slowly crept into the dark zone.

In the dark zone, there was no light. I hugged the walls until I reached Bradley Cooper. He had a giant bite mark on his thigh, which made it impossible for him to walk. I refused to leave him behind and threw his body over my shoulders like a firefighter carrying the dead weight of a human that had inhaled too much smoke. On the way out of the cave, I heard a man yell, "Wait!"

When I turned around, Zach Galifianakis was striding out of the twilight. He had the same yellow eyes as the big ass werewolf and a matching beard. Zach Galifinakis asked, "Where are you going? You just got here." I was confused and thought, "He saw me? He saw the big ass werewolf, and did not try to help?" Upon seeing my pensive expression, Zach Galifinakis started to laugh. His body shuddered as the laughter grew louder and louder and louder until he transformed into a big ass werewolf. It was the sexiest transformation I had ever seen.

My heart was racing, not because I was scared, but because I was intrigued. I ran my hand through his coarse fur, which felt like sand. The body beneath was producing so much heat that I started sweating. I tried to tell Zach Galifinakis to bite me, but he ran off in the opposite direction, leaving me behind with Bradley Cooper, who at that point was crying and asking "Oh my God, what is happening?"

I asked myself that same question and wished that I had the courage to chase Zach Galifanakis into the night, to run free until the break of day. Instead, I carried Bradley Cooper approximately three miles to the emergency room.

Before I left, he told me to be careful. "It is a strange world out there," he said. "It is easy to get lost in the moment." Bradley Cooper's words echoed in my head as I walked back to the forest, where I found Zach Galifinakis running through the trees, lost in the moment. It truly was just that easy.

Sharing One Brief and Savage Wilderness

Jennifer Lawrence and I entered a virtual reality simulation of post-apocalyptic America shortly following an extreme change of climate that claimed the lives of ninety-nine percent of the population. It was quite frightening. Jennifer Lawrence and I ran wild through the woods behind my childhood home, imagining we were the last two people on Earth.

We passed the infamous frozen lake that I fell into one winter. No. Wait. She fell in. We used our outdoor voices, with no regard for the secrets we let loose through the trees. Burs stuck to our clothes. Thorns ripped apart our summer skin. We clambered up a tangled tree and hid between the branches. "Who can climb higher?" It was never I. I threw tantrums, usually: the sore loser, in tears, selfish and immature.

Sitting moodily on one of the limbs, I was unaware of the beast that was approaching below, its chest ripped wide open, like an opened blood orange, oozing juicy and delicious nectar. Jennifer Lawrence's glossy marble eyes stared. The beast was one of my neighbor's hunting dogs. As a child, I remember seeing it rip a gentle deer apart at its seams.

Jennifer Lawrence approached the beast with the gentleness of a lamb. The beast howled, but Jennifer Lawrence continued forward. She pressed her hand against its damp fur and hummed as the gory dog slowly collapsed onto the ground, allowing her to seal the wound on its chest. I said, "You are saving a predator! As soon as it is healthy again, it will try to tear you to shreds." She told me to have faith.

When she was finished sewing up the beast, it stood back up and licked Jennifer Lawrence playfully. A fawn sprang out from behind the trees, and the beast smiled. It bounded around the fawn, rejuvenated, and licked the fawn with the same fondness that it licked Jennifer Lawrence. Then, with one swift motion of its claws, the beast ripped the gentle fawn apart at its seams. Its bloody face turned to me, dripping crimson, still smiling.

"Run!" Jennifer Lawrence yelled, but it was too late. I knew from my childhood, once the beast was after you, there was no escape. I said, "No, you are way more gifted than me in your respective field. Leave me, and get away!" Right as the beast lunged toward me, Jennifer Lawrence pulled out a gun and shot the beast in its back. It lay still for a while, and everything in the forest seemed silent.

Then, as soon as the beast stopped breathing, a whole family of deer ran out from behind different trees to do unspeakable things to its remains. Jennifer Lawrence said, "It never pays to be a martyr," and ran toward the deer as if they were a flock of birds, dispersing them in all directions so that the beast could lie in peace, and pieces, side by side. Then we left the virtual reality simulation, and reentered reality, where we both said, "That was extraordinarily sad."

The More Relaxed You Are, the Better You Are at Everything

I was on a fishing trip with Bill Murray in Alaska, having a jolly time when we stumbled upon a bizarre sight. There was a birch tree covered in an indeterminate amount of slender, cylindrical flowers without petals. We stood there for a while admiring the flowers' beauty when all of the sudden Bill Murray spotted something moving in the shadows.

That something turned out to be an alpha moose. In fact, there was an entire herd of angry moose in the darkness that had been seeking revenge against humans since the Stone Age.

About a minute later another moose appeared, then another, then another. Bill Murray and I started backing into the tall grass behind us without thinking about the fact that we were garnishing ourselves with plants that these herbivores loved to eat. I followed Bill Murray down into a little ravine because he thought we could hide there, but when I looked around, there was dark fur on the trees, hairy piles of poop on the ground, holes dug in the dirt.

There was a series of eerie grunts from at least ten different moose circling on higher ground, and I knew then that we were in their den. A moment later, there were two moose galloping on a full tilt with their antlers projected directly toward us. I wanted to run, but I was totally stunned. It was a do or die situation, and I was ready to die.

I thought that the antlers would skewer us both, but just then Bill Murray made a noise that sounded something like a tire skid, and a pig squealing. The moose slid to a halt with fear in their eyes. Bill Murray made the noise again, then again. The moose turned around, terrified of Bill Murray, and ran back up the hill to warn the other moose to retreat.

It was bone chilling. We were lucky that moose couldn't count, or else we would have been dead for sure. They would have known that there were only two of us, with zero weapons, and that their herd could have easily stampeded us to death like the wildebeest did to Mufasa. What shocked me the most was that Bill Murray had not stopped smiling during the entire encounter.

He smiled when we came upon the birch tree. He smiled when we saw the alpha moose. He smiled when we heard the eerie grunts, and he smiled when a quartet of antlers nearly impaled us. He smiled while he squealed, and he smiled when the moose turned tail and ran. It was zen, and totally hard-core at the same time.

People Come into This World as a Teeny Wrinkled-Up Fetus and Leave Possessed by Ghosts

I took a walk through the deep dark woods with David Lynch. David Lynch kept remarking on how the wind felt like silk sliding against his cheekbones, and how the humidity felt like a velvet scarf wrapped around his neck. He said that the pristine weather had something to do with Jupiter and Saturn aligning. I was too busy worrying about the owls to respond. I'd had an irrational fear of owls ever since witnessing a great horned owl pecking a possum's eyes out in the alley behind my house. David Lynch kept saying, "The owls are not what they seem." They seemed like feathered demons.

They were actually the guardians of the deep dark woods, omnipresent and always watching. I thought I heard one hoot, but it was just David Lynch coughing as he smoked a cigarette. The path we were walking ended in a grove marked with stones that formed a circle in the center. There was evil lurking all around us. I could feel it. I'd felt it in my dreams before. The air smelled like scorched motor lubricant and hung over us like heavy-duty cotton fabric. David Lynch said that we were standing at the entrance to the Black Lodge and that fear was the only way to enter. I said, "Mission accomplished."

I was actually kind of pissed off. I was hungry, and David Lynch told me that we would go to PF Chang's on our walk back to the car. He didn't say anything about a pit stop at a portal to another dimension that just so happened to be a realm governed by the malevolent. I felt like Frodo and wished I had Gandalf or Sam to back me up instead of an old man chain-smoking and talking endlessly about the climate.

While I was pouting, Billy Ray Cyrus appeared out of the Black Lodge with a revolver aimed at David Lynch and a deranged smile on his face. Apparently, Billy Ray Cyrus blamed David Lynch for leading his daughter Miley Cyrus astray and turning her into the Disney-manufactured pop sensation that was Hannah Montana. David Lynch said that the Devil was responsible for all Disney-associated acts and that he would not be held accountable.

Billy Ray Cyrus didn't answer. He was still smiling and hadn't blinked for more than a minute before taking a shot at David Lynch's head with his pistol. David Lynch ducked and dodged the bullet, but Billy Ray Cyrus tackled him to the ground. I grabbed Billy Ray Cyrus by the mullet and pulled him off of David Lynch with all my strength.

I dragged Billy Ray Cyrus back to the Black Lodge, sacrificing myself so that David Lynch could escape. If there was one person who needed to keep contributing their work to the world, it was David Lynch.

The Black Lodge was a very scary place, with very scary people, and all I remembered from my time there was a lot of screaming, and the whites of Billy Ray Cyrus' eyes staring blankly into my soul. Sometimes when I looked in the mirror, I could his face and could hear the whirring drone of Achy Breaky Heart in the back of my mind. Sometimes I wanted to smash my face against the mirror but resisted the urge. I knew that's what Billy Ray Cyrus would want. I wasn't going to give him the satisfaction.

"I wish I could do whatever I liked behind the curtain of madness. Then: I'd arrange flowers, all day long, I'd paint; pain, love and tenderness, I would laugh as much as I feel like at the stupidity of others, and they would all say: "Poor thing, she's crazy!" (Above all I would laugh at my own stupidity.) I would build my world which while I lived, would be in agreement with all the worlds. The day, or the hour, or the minute that I lived would be mine and everyone else's - my madness would not be an escape from reality."

— Frida Kahlo

Megalomania Is a Psychopathological Condition Characterized by Fantasies of Power and Inflation

I went over Kanye West's house to hang out and somehow ended up in outer space. Kanye West said that his music got people high, but I didn't realize he meant all the way to the sky. Then again, a different album of his was playing in every room of the house. In the bedroom, he was playing My Beautiful Dark Twisted Fantasy. In the bathroom, he was playing Cruel Summer. He offered me banana pudding in the kitchen while we listened to The Life of Pablo. Then we drank liquor and bumped Yeezus on the balcony.

It was at this point that we started to float away from the house, hovering above it until Kanye West told his kids' nanny to "Turn the fucking speakers up." His daughter North was in his arms, and he kept saying, "I love traveling North with North," and "We're on top of the world, baby!" in a manic auto-tuned voice. I told Kanye West that we were floating east, and he looked at me as if I had just spat in his face. He screamed, "This is my universe! You just exist in it! We're going in whatever direction I say!" I could tell that he was scaring his daughter, so I said, "Okay, Kanye." He smiled, and responded, "Hey, that's a pretty good rhyme!" I had no idea if he was being sarcastic or not, but it didn't matter. The loud music drowned out the rest of his rant, though his mouth continued moving for our entire trip to outer space and back.

By the time we floated down, Kanye West had lost his voice. He didn't even give a goodbye gesture before I was escorted out by one of his bodyguards, who apparently couldn't talk either. It was one of Kanye West's rules, and there were cameras all around the house to make sure none of the bodyguards spoke to anyone or did anything except for bobbing their heads to the music, and protect Kanye West in the case of an emergency. When I was about to turn toward my car, the bodyguard pretended to sneeze. Then, covering his mouth so that the cameras couldn't see, he mouthed the words, "Help me," without a moment's pause from head bobbing. I nodded to him reassuringly and then drove away from the house as fast as I could.

Adopting Progressive Ideals to Protect Future Generations (Think of the Children)

I was in an underground casino that only the Illuminati were allowed in. I was Illuminati purely by association as the babysitter of Brad Pitt and Angelina Jolie's kids. Brangelina said that they wanted to show their children what their parents did for a living. Their children were all well behaved, especially compared to Will Smith's kids, who were dancing on top of pool tables for attention, tearing up the felt with the heels of their shoes.

After losing thirty straight hands of poker, Brangelina was beginning to look frustrated. This was just the warm-up, though. The real action was in the high-stakes black market section of the casino. While we were walking over, I spotted George Clooney approaching from a distance. His teeth looked like pearls in the iridescent slot machine glow. Brangelina and George Clooney locked eyes, striding toward one another with clenched fists and pursed lips.

They met in front of a foosball table in the center of the high-stakes black market section of the casino. George Clooney challenged Brangelina to a game to eleven, wagering his villa in Italy, in return for their Chateau Miraval, pre-Roman estate.

Brangelina turned down this offer and came up with an alternative bet. They offered their six children in exchange for George Clooney's serene seven thousand three hundred and fifty-four square foot home in Los Angeles. I objected, but it was too late. George Clooney agreed to their terms, and the game was on.

It was two against one, but George Clooney's hands were as nimble as they come. He flicked his wrist with such finesse that the score was five to nothing within a minute of the match's start. Brangelina looked as if they had lost already by the looks on their sad, drooping faces. Their kids had no idea what was going on, in fact, they were cheering for George Clooney because kids naturally like to see their parents humiliated by strangers.

George Clooney used his momentum and scored five more points in the next minute so that he only needed one more to win. Brangelina got one point when George Clooney scored on himself out of pity. The final goal was a brutal snakeshot that left Brangelina staring at the table in awe, both of their arrogance and of George Clooney's skill. It was super awkward to watch, as was George Clooney's speech to the children where he declared himself their new father.

He kept stressing how he never wanted to have kids because the world is such a fucked up place, and he didn't want to subject his children to an inevitable life of severe depression due to a lack of any kind of promising future.

As he said this, though, there was an atmospheric shift, and out of the shadows, a figure appeared, glowing and radiant like a sunrise over the ocean. The figure was Bernie Sanders, with his signature sidekick Birdie Sanders sitting on his shoulder. Bernie Sanders stood between Brangelina's kids and George Clooney, who began to hiss and posture like a serpent.

Bernie Sanders held his finger out and began to wag it while explaining to George Clooney how his attitude was perpetuating a negative stereotype that enabled bad behavior. George Clooney cowered in fear and covered his ears as if he were a demon hearing Bible passages read by a priest. Bernie Sanders was relentless, driving George Clooney back until the silver fox fled through the Russian roulette section, narrowly dodging a bullet that flew past his tail.

Brangelina thanked Bernie Sanders for his services, and after some whispering asked him if he would consider raising their children for them. Bernie Sanders smiled a toothy grin and agreed on the condition that Brangelina becomes environmental activists to promote policies that will help combat climate change.

Brangelina accepted, but they stipulated that Hillary Rodham Clinton was still going to be their nominee for president of the United States. Bernie Sanders sighed, and said "Whatever." He looked over at the kids and started smiling again, and walked them out of the underground casino to his Subaru Outback on the surface.

I followed them, looking back at the last moment to see Jon Voight asking Brangelina where his grandchildren were. The scene made me cringe like a mouthful of sour warheads, and I couldn't watch anymore. I ran after Bernie Sanders, hoping that some of his trailing positivity might rub off on me.

Being around Bernie Sanders was as refreshing as meditation, as liberating as yoga, and as energizing as a quartz crystal. I wanted him to adopt me too, but I was too old for that. I settled for following him on tour like a groupie, watching him caution the people about the world's warning signs with his ever-growing family by his side.

Deconstructing Reality and Mounting Levels of Insanity at the Illuminati Party

I went to the best party on Earth at Beyoncé and Jay-Z's mansion. It was me, the cast of Boy Meets World, and a hundred of the most beautiful people I'd ever seen. The first thing that I noticed though was the buffet. There was a fountain in the center oozing lobster butter, surrounded by all kinds of exotic animals to eat. I examined the condor omelet bar with skepticism. The guy shaving giraffe meat kept looking at me like I was the weird one.

A chemist in a laboratory coat approached me and asked if I wanted to try any of his psychedelics. When I asked him what kind he had, the chemist told me that I could say whatever type of psychedelic I wanted, and he would make it in front of me. I asked him for something mellow with a euphoric peak, and no crash.

He cooked with all kinds of herbs and powders, and the result was an unappetizing gray blob. It tasted terrible, but I immediately felt better after eating it. All I needed to do was pee, and I would be at perfect peace with the world.

The chemist told me that the bathroom was down the hall to the right, but I was too high and accidentally made a left. I walked down some steps and opened the door. What I thought was a bathroom turned out to be a basement filled children, specifically, the Kidz Bop kids. They were crying into boiling cauldrons that were labeled "the cure." I started crying too when I realized the suffering and pain that was happening in secret.

When I went back upstairs, it started to make sense. Beyoncé and Jay-Z's sound system, for example, had graphics of an Egyptian pyramid, with a hieroglyphic that had light flowing through it on the sides. There were bizarre, esoteric symbols all over the walls and ceiling as well. The center of the floor even had an all-seeing eye carved into it. From this evidence, I concluded that the house was an Illuminati sweatshop that occasionally hosted outlandishly indulgent parties for its members.

I was bewildered, and tripping hard on whatever psychedelic the chemist had made when Ben Savage from Boy Meets World tried to grab Beyoncé's ass. It was unusually lewd behavior for Ben Savage, and the fact that I shared a name with a potential pervert made me feel ever worse. I was on my way to a full-blown bad trip until out of nowhere someone screamed "Dragon!"

Actually, nobody screamed "Dragon!" It was a hallucination from the psychedelics that induced my fight or flight instinct. I ran out screaming, past the palm trees, under the arches, and out of the gate. My car was parked back at the mansion, but I didn't care. I was trying to escape a dragon. So I kept running until I was home, occasionally looking over my shoulder to see a fiery sky slowly growing closer.

Developing Neurophysiological Distinctions to Rewire the Brain

I was a bit skeptical about parties following my incident with the dragon, but when Taylor Swift invited me to her twenty-second birthday party in the Hollywood Hills, I couldn't refuse. I decided to drive up with Ed Sheeran because he seemed like an extraordinarily nice guy.

Our first encounter couldn't have been more awkward. I mistook Ed Sheeran for Rupert Grint, and wouldn't let him into my car until he showed me proper identification. Ed Sheeran smiled patiently and said, "I am a polite, compassionate man, gracious and kind in every way. You just can't see it through your tinted window." Eventually, I let him in, and the first thing that he did was rub down the passenger's seat with wet wipes from KFC.

I drove us to the bottom of the hill, and we took a shuttle the rest of the way. When we reached our destination at the top, the view of Los Angeles was mind-blowing. It looked like a screenshot from Blade Runner. Taylor Swift's house had three hundred sixty degrees of windows overlooking the city and beyond, like an observatory that you had to take an open-air elevator to reach, from which the passengers could view a ten story tall monument of Taylor Swift that was made entirely of bronze.

The only foods served at the party were mustard-roasted fish, gluten-free pizza, thinly sliced ham, and cookie dough. The beverage options were diet coke, orange juice, and pumpkin-spice lattes. Luckily I'd eaten one of Captain Kirk's Oklahoma Sweet Cakes, a cannabis-infused edible, just before coming to the party, so all I wanted to eat was cookie dough, and all I wanted to drink was orange juice.

I was in the middle of asking Ed Sheeran if I had any chocolate chip residue between my teeth when Taylor Swift started singing her new song 22. It was apparently an alternative to the birthday song and was strange because everybody at the party except for me immediately stopped talking and started taking pictures of Taylor Swift's impromptu performance.

Ed Sheeran took out his camera phone and filmed the entire four minutes, without pausing from staring at the screen once to look up. I was a bit panicked and nudged Katy Perry, who also appeared disturbed. She shrugged it off and pretended to dance while I continued to gawk in horror by how manufactured the scene looked.

While the guests ate birthday cake and took turns liking each other's recently posted photos of Taylor Swift on Instagram, I took the elevator back downstairs to use the only bathroom in the entire house. I apparently went one floor too far and ended up in the basement.

What I saw underground shocked me, but didn't shock me at the same time. It was the Kidz Bop kids, different ones than I'd seen in Jay-Z and Beyoncé's basement. There were coloring books, crayons, dolls, action figures, and board games all around the room, but none of the Kidz Bop kids looked happy. In fact, they all looked old and tired, like their youth was gone. I realized then that Taylor Swift was actually the Pied Piper, and had dragged the kids to her dungeon so that she could feed on their innocence and drain their ingenuity.

I immediately left the party and went to the LAPD to tell them about everything that I had seen. Nobody believed me. Ultimately, one of the off-duty officers volunteered to take a ride to the house with me purely in the interest of getting Taylor Swift's autograph for his daughter. The odd thing was that when we got back, the house was empty. In fact, there was no evidence that anyone had ever been there. I swore to the off-duty officer that my testimony was true, but he just shook his head and drove off without me.

It was as soon as he turned the corner and went out of view that from over the hill I saw the army of the night appear, led by Ed Sheeran. It was made up of over a thousand tweens fortified with farming equipment similar to the kids in Children of the Corn. They were chanting "Hail Taylor, hail the chosen one." Ed Sheeran bellowed, "Seize the outlander!"

The army of the night sprinted down the hill at breakneck speed, and I was their only target. I heard a whirring sound descending from overhead, and looked up to see a helicopter hovering above me. Katy Perry was the captain and tossed down a ladder that I was able to grab just as Ed Sheeran came rushing towards me with a pitchfork. One of the prongs caught me in my ankle, and I gave him the middle finger as Katy Perry flew me to safety.

She set us down on top of Children's Hospital Los Angeles using a slick landing maneuver, then helped me hobble inside so that a nurse could bandage the pitchfork wound on my leg. When we were in the waiting room, though, something didn't feel right. I felt the eyes of the children around us, staring at Katy Perry and me with animosity. They climbed out of their chairs with irreverent frowns, creeping and crawling toward us as the LED lights flickered.

I thought that they were going to murder us, but then something happened that I didn't expect. Katy Perry started singing. She sang her song Firework, dancing around the room while she looked into the eyes of the children. Slowly the color came back into their eyes, and the neutrality to their faces. Some of them even started to dance along to the music, gamboling and giggling as she sang, "Boom, boom, boom, even brighter than the moon, moon, moon!"

Katy Perry sang the rest of her Teenage Dream album until every child in the hospital was cured. The sun rose on the horizon with the realization that these children are not truly an army of darkness, but good kids who were having their innocence warped by an eerie trickster. Music was not music. Adult brains could not process high-pitched frequencies. Only the ears of canines and children were sensitive to the manipulation of sound. I was glad that I was too old to become a prop, though it seemed that many others in the industry were not.

When Katy Perry finished singing, I asked her what we could do to get the message out about Taylor Swift's influence over adolescents. She shook her head and responded, "There are some forces in this world beyond our control." Then she said, "I see everything through a spiritual lens." I understood then that in some ways, Katy Perry had performed a musical exorcism on the children possessed by Taylor Swift, and maybe that was the answer.

A quote mistakenly attributed to Plato once said, "Music is a moral law. It gives soul to the universe, wings to the mind, flight to the imagination, and charm and gaiety to life and everything." I knew this was true and was determined to spread the message to the next generation. Music could save the people from themselves; all they needed to do was listen.

Myths and Exaggerations Form to Frighten Vulnerable People

I inadvertently joined a cult that I found via Craigslist in an attempt to meet new people and forge new relationships. The cult was called the Serene Order and did not present itself as a cult, but rather a body of religious beliefs. Their ad said they would be meeting for a retreat at the end of the month, and that anyone was welcome to join.

When I got there, Tom Cruise greeted me at the entrance and asked that I relinquish any personal belongings for the remainder of my stay. Tom Cruise said, "This will be a pilgrimage of paradoxes, a journey of the ins and outs, pleasure and pain, relaxation and tension. Out of your most awful fears, you will gain strength." I liked the way Tom Cruise spoke, mistaking his charisma for sincerity.

"You will never tire of this journey. We will move together, changing speeds as we go, faster than a beam of light, slower than a turtle's pace. You will experience many parts of yourself," said Tom Cruise, "and all of your experiences will be in the here and now. Each moment is a unique and precious thing and yours for the taking."

When the other newcomers gathered, there were around a hundred people total; Tom Cruise opened with a speech on responsibility. He said, "Repeat after me. You are not responsible for my feelings." The newcomers and I repeated, "I am not responsible for your feelings," again and again until they believed it to be absolute truth.

Tom Cruise said, "You perceive me from your place, and not as I am. I perceive myself not in the reflection of your perception, but in the full experience of my being. If you do not like me, it changes me not, your dislike belongs to you and is not part of me."

That night, Tom Cruise took the newcomers on a hike to the bottom of a nearby valley that was steep, rocky, and covered with trees. As the sun set, I became fearful and thought "what if," and "maybe," and "I can't see in the dark," and "I won't make it out of this valley." Tom Cruise said, "Look to your fear to gain strength," and I did.

Little by little my eyes were adjusted until I could see again, and realized I was not alone. I became aware of how many choices there were in life, each and every one of which was mine to make.

For the first time, I became conscious of a power within myself that I had never felt before. "But power," I thought, "what kind of person would want to be powerful?" I was afraid that it would scare everyone away. All I wanted was the permission to be myself.

Hiking up the steep, rocky hill made me feel like I was moving incredibly slow, almost to the point that I could no longer perceive any forward motion. Then I stopped breathing for a moment before starting again, feeling both pleasure and pain surge inside of me as I began to self-actualize. I said, "No one is responsible for me but me. I am alone. I am separate. I can get what I need at my own pace, and in my own time, in my own way. I do not have to take this path unless I have chosen to do so."

When we reached camp, I ingested chemical drugs for the first time in the form of LSD. During the trip, I was renamed Goose by Tom Cruise, and given the guidelines to living in the Serene Order. Since it was Monday, Tom Cruise informed me that Monday was confession, a ceremony where each person confessed his or her wrongdoings for the past week. The punishments were passed down by Tom Cruise based on the degree of the offense committed. For example, Tom Cruise told me about a time when one man was beaten with a belt for over an hour after stealing a jacket from another man during one of their evening bonfires. I reassured Tom Cruise that I wanted to be a good disciple, and he smiled maniacally.

When I asked Tom Cruise about how the Serene Order formed, Tom Cruise gave him a speech about the discovery of electricity. He spoke about how monumental the impact was on the way humans viewed their reality, and how the inventions that followed caused people to fear for their lives. He told me that I needed to accept my place in the Serene Order so that I could harness my true potential.

I was beginning to feel like I'd finally found a place where I belong, just as the police arrived to raid their camp. It turned out that Tom Cruise was actually a con artist who was traveling state-to-state recruiting followers that he could easily dose and manipulate into donating their life savings to him. The police arrest him on a slew of charges, including attempted homicide from allegedly planting explosives under the car of one of his former followers who'd threatened to turn him in.

I felt like a tourist who climbed an old piece of architecture to take in the view for a few minutes before turning back, with a way of seeing the world that was keenly aware but still superficial and transient. I learned a great deal from my week with Tom Cruise but wondered if any of it was real, or if I had been taken advantage of without realizing. The police seemed to think the latter and told me that I was lucky they'd gotten there when they did before Tom Cruise irreversibly scrambled my brain.

Then the police showed me a video of a man in a stark kitchen who asked if there was anyone out there who still wasn't clear about what doing drugs does. He held up an egg and said, "This is your brain," before indicating a frying pan and adding, "This is drugs." He then cracked open the shell, fried the egg, and said, "This is your brain on drugs." He stared at his audience and asked, "Any questions?"

"The great proof of madness is the disproportion of one's designs to one's means."

— Napoleon Bonaparte

Make America Nonexistent Again

A series of secret service men pulled me into the back of an unusually long limousine to speak with their boss. I was barely able to fit because most of the luxury sedan was taken up by a slug-like alien known as Donald Trump. I was shocked because I always thought Donald Trump was an average sized man. It turned out that the human Donald Trump appearing at presidential rallies was only a hologram, and that the real Donald Trump was more horrible than anyone could have possibly imagined.

Donald Trump told me that he needed my connections to the criminal underground to replace his current employees, a retinue of crooked businesspeople, bounty hunters, smugglers, assassins and bodyguards, which he used to operate his presidential campaign. When I asked him why, Donald Trump told me that the only person he could trust was his son Eric Trump, whose greatest traits were also morbid obesity and corruption.

I told Donald Trump that this was a big misunderstanding. He responded that if I didn't give him what he wanted, I would be fed to his Rancor, which I thought was just an imaginary creature from Star Wars. In reality, the Rancor was a semi-sentient reptilian predator that Donald Trump captured from outer space. I could hear it growling from the limousine's enormous trunk.

The one thing that Donald Trump didn't have, though, was space to move. So I began to tickle him. I tickled Donald Trump's belly, then moved up to his armpits and neck. His laughter was so violent that the entire limousine flipped over in front of the Empire State Building.

I made my way out of the car before its engine exploded, but Donald Trump was not so lucky. His blubber was blown across the block, sticking all over the sidewalk and street signs. The Rancor made it out in time and climbed the Empire State Building like King Kong before being ironically shot down by one of Donald Trump's drones. When Donald Trump's secret service saw me, I tried to run away. One of the agents got to me first and held out a card that granted me a one-year supply of Trump Steaks.

I'd heard nothing but good things about Trump Steaks, and they were apparently all that Donald Trump ingested while he was alive, other than the tears of the Kidz Bop kids and crust from the cracked scabs of his laborers. Donald Trump's secret service agent told me to enjoy myself, but to be careful, "The label may say beef, but it's one hundred percent horsemeat."

An Irresistible–Uncontrollable Impulse, Resulting in Excessive, Expensive and Time-Consuming Retail Activity

Barack Obama started a campaign at Starbucks so that every time someone bought a bag of coffee an American got a job. I bought a hundred bags of decaf and thought about how beautiful the corporate model of charity was. From that moment on, I pledged to cope with my depression through spontaneous consumer choices instead of overeating.

My favorite time to buy stuff was around four or five in the morning on the shopping network. For example, I got a glandular dopamine burst from procuring a worthless doctorate from a for-profit college. Then I saw that Barack Obama started a cleaning product company where every product was buy one get three free. I purchased a lifetime supply from the president and got a video of him faking me out with his famous left-handed double pump shot for only a hundred dollars extra.

When I got home, I cleaned my house until it was devoid of bacteria, which caused me to form an immune deficiency on top of the superiority complex that I'd developed from all of the money that I'd spent on certificates and orphan education. Because of my addiction, I'd forgotten that the key to life was to value my time. My life energy was worth like a billion dollars an hour, and I was done wasting it.

I had three cases of Sylvester Stallone's High Protein Pudding that were inedible, as were Hulk Hogan's Hulkster Burgers. Charities wouldn't even take them as donations because the taste was so revolting. I decided to give everything away to the San Diego Zoo because they said that the food could nourish the gorillas, which had stomachs made of steel. In return, the San Diego Zoo supplied me with a lifetime pass and a satchel with a lemur logo on it.

I decided to visit the zoo with my niece for her birthday one weekend and was shocked by what we saw in the gorilla house. We saw Arnold Schwarzenegger crawling around on his hands and knees. He was wearing a burlap sack, and I'm pretty sure that he had lice. He had two fistfuls of Sylvester Stallone's High Protein Pudding and was rubbing it all over the walls and his chest. I realized then that the universe was trying to tell me something. It was saying that the key to life was giving up on the notion that time or the things that I did matter.

Battle of the Alpha Males

I was working as a nightshift manager for Planet Fitness when Michael Moore asked if he could do a documentary on what life was like in a gym environment. I told him that I'd be more than happy to let him film as long as none of the members had a problem with it. Of course, none of them did. Most tried to pose purposefully and flex in front of the camera, even when it wasn't recording.

It didn't take long for Michael Moore to find a nemesis in the form of a YouTube fitness personality who thought Michael Moore's inferior camera tripod was "laughable." The YouTube fitness personality wasn't even working out. He mostly just walked around with his shirt off, periodically pouring water on his head so that he looked incredibly sweaty as if he'd just finished an intense session. Michael Moore asked the YouTube fitness personality how he shaped his body without actually lifting weights. The YouTube fitness personality responded that he sculpts his physique with an aggressive fat loss program that involves chain-smoking cigarettes and drinking ten cups of coffee with every meal.

Things took a sour turn when the YouTube fitness personality started whipping Michael Moore's stomach with his damp, sleeveless shirt, telling him that he needed to get to the gym more often. Michael Moore retorted that the YouTube fitness personality was probably the kid at school who would use the manual pencil sharpener just to flex his muscles for the girls in class to see. He asked the YouTube fitness personality how his superficial approach was working with the ladies these days, and proceeded to show clips that he filmed of twenty different women in the gym appearing perturbed by the YouTube fitness personality's invasive motivational speaking that he shot on his camera phone while strutting around the gym.

The YouTube fitness personality was getting humiliated by all of Michael Moore's well-timed jokes, and with no comeback, all he could do was mock Michael Moore's laugh. They chuckled back and forth at one another until the YouTube fitness personality could not take anymore and began to cry like a bully who'd been stood up to for the first time and exposed as nothing more than an insecure poser with no real substance to his intimidation.

Michael Moore's documentary culminated in a scene where the YouTube fitness personality smashed his camera in the parking lot, a physical manifestation of his mental breakdown. Michael Moore was simultaneously filming selfie style with his smartphone, and included a clip following the credits of him laughing as he said, "Let that be a lesson to you all, exercise will make you go insane."

I was disturbed that this was the message Michael Moore was sending out to the world but didn't interject in fear that he would roast me the way he did the YouTube fitness personality. I kept my mouth shut, and I regretted it, because, despite the fact that the YouTube fitness personality was the biggest jerk I'd ever met, he wasn't an accurate representation of the workout community. A better depiction would be someone like Carrot Top, who got huge in the gym through hard work and HGH injections. He came out looking like a monster from a horror film in the eighties, which is why I thought that Michael Moore's documentary would have been better as a psychological thriller than a comedy. In the end, though, it was his vision, and I could do nothing about it except smile and pray that people would recognize me from standing in the background of his footage.

A Grueling Continuum of Normalcy

It took me three tries to pass my driver's test. On my first try, I forgot how to parallel park. On my second try, Thom Yorke was assigned to be my instructor. I did well for the first few stoplights, slowing down without slamming on the break, signaling, and staying within the speed limit. Then Thom Yorke told me to make a right where I should have made a left. I drove right into the parking lot of a prison labor camp hidden behind a billboard that said, "Eat Organic or Die."

Thom Yorke held me against my will and forced me to make tortillas for underprivileged Kidz Bop kids while he sang Karma Police over the loudspeaker. I felt intense shame. I met Antonio Banderas on the assembly line. He hugged me and smelled like the ocean. When his shift ended, Antonio Banderas offered to stay on with me. We worked in a tiny room for a very long time. Antonio Banderas told me about his childhood. His life was very dull, but I enjoyed the company.

A loud siren signaled the end of my shift, and I sat on the floor, exhausted and hungry. I had only been working for an hour or so, but I hadn't eaten breakfast, or gotten much sleep the night before. Thom Yorke would not release me, even when I told him that I was a diabetic who needed insulin to survive. Antonio Banderas said that he knew a secret way out, through a revolving door behind Thom Yorke's guitar amp, but he was too scared to attempt an escape. So when Thom Yorke left the compound to give another unsuspecting victim their driver's test, I decided to make a run for it. Antonio Banderas asked me if I would go to the police station, and bring back help. I told him my house was in the opposite direction, and that I already had a long enough walk ahead of me without any pit stops. I made it out of the prison labor camp alive, and for my entire walk home, thought about how much easier it would be to get back if I had a car.

On my third driver's test, the instructor was a conservative racist. It seemed that the motor vehicle bureau had gone in a very different direction since Thom Yorke's arrest for manufacturing an illegal sweatshop. The conservative racist gave me my license based on the color of my skin alone, but I took the test anyway and parallel parked like an absolute champ. That was the day I decided to give up driving for public transportation.

People on the bus were typically friendly and kept their radical beliefs to themselves.

An Opportunity to Liberate from Someone Else's Destructive Design of the World

I entered the matrix to visit Keanu Reeves. He'd become quite soft spoken since moving to a simulated reality in the dystopian future. Keanu Reeves told me that he'd given up on life, and was ready to offer his bodies' heat and electrical activity as energy to the sentient machines that controlled the universe. His goal was to become a corpse that the sentient machines spoke through, with no ego, nothing inside of him except for love. He was impossible to offend, very sweet, and funny in an ironic way.

I had attempted to find a healthy mind-space, to live in the moment, but thought about the past too much. I was still angry with the guy who looked at me weird when we were stopped at an intersection that morning. I wanted to give up on the past and the future, to live freely in a dream world.

Keanu Reeves said that the illusions of law, order, and authority were all created to keep humans trapped by moral obligations, which as a result made freedom itself a deception. I laughed and told him that he should take his comedy routine on the road.

Keanu Reeves owned a white rabbit that he claimed was River Phoenix reincarnated. He'd found the matrix in the first place by following River Phoenix, and said that the rabbit was responsible for saving him from his depressing existence on Earth. Then he told me that he'd spent his entire life typecast as some sort of savior. All he wanted to do was spend time with River Phoenix, painting Chinese symbols on the walls for the rest of eternity.

When I asked what his philosophy was, Keanu Reeves responded, "I'm very spiritual, supremely spiritual, bountifully spiritual, and supremely bountiful." I nodded at his wisdom.

Since I couldn't say anything to convince Keanu Reeves to come back with me, I decided to steal River Phoenix so that he might be lured back with us. I ran over and picked the rabbit up in my arms. River Phoenix bit my hand as hard as he could with his two front teeth, but I blocked out the pain.

It wasn't until I reentered reality that I realized Keanu Reeves had not followed us back. He was too far-gone, on a remote network that most people could not comprehend. Maybe one day Keanu Reeves will reappear, shaggy and even paler. Until then, I had River Phoenix for companionship, though he kept quiet under the coffee table most days, trying to dig through the floor to another dimension.

"But what is liberty without wisdom, and without virtue? It is the greatest of all possible evils; for it is folly, vice, and madness, without tuition or restraint."

— Edmund Burke

The Pain of Catharsis is Always in Service of Elevating to Some Higher Plane of Being

I was assigned to interview David Hasselhoff for the school newspaper. I started by asking him about his life. David Hasselhoff told me that I could understand his life by looking inside of his refrigerator. His refrigerator was empty. Before I could respond, he said "Exactly," and lifted up his shirt to display a set of gleaming abdominal muscles. He told me that taste was inbred in him. I was not sure what that meant. I asked David Hasselhoff what it was like to work on Baywatch. He replied, "Horny." He was totally alpha, and more than a little drunk. His jokes were consistently bad, but not as bad as his breath.

By the end of the interview, I wanted to be David Hasselhoff. It was something about his ability to not give a fuck about anything, which was very appealing to me. There I was, laboring over an interview that made me miserable while David Hasselhoff sat at his kitchen table eating a stack of waffles that was far beyond the caloric intake required for any normal human being to be satisfied. I was fairly sure that he had no plans to exercise either. Not to mention, the man looked stunning for a sixty-year-old alcoholic. At my stress rate, I'd be lucky to live that long.

David Hasselhoff must have picked up on my melancholy because he offered me a warm beer and a cigar. I was only sixteen. After our third round, I asked David Hasselhoff if he would take a selfie with me. We held our beers up to the camera like frat bros, cigars in our mouths like gangsters or famous athletes. I showed everyone I knew. The editor of the school newspaper even agreed to put the picture on the front page of the next issue.

Then one afternoon I was called into Principal O'Shaughnessy's office, and asked a series of questions about my interview with David Hasselhoff. Principal O'Shaughnessy kept reiterating that I was not in any trouble. Up until that point, I had never been disciplined at school. I had never received a demerit or skipped a day of classes. Principal O'Shaughnessy thanked me for my cooperation and suggested that I should stay away from bad influences, especially the older ones.

About a week later the school newspaper printed another story about David Hasselhoff, about how the police arrested him for distributing alcohol and tobacco to an unspecified student of Roman Catholic High School. According to the article, when the police found David Hasselhoff, he was lying on the floor, trying to eat a cheeseburger without the use of his hands. The lead investigator described his body movements as "wormlike."

His wife left him following the scandal. He was denied child visitation privilege because his crime involved a minor. After ninety days in treatment, he moved back to Los Angeles, where he could once again bodysurf, and live by the water in peace. I no longer wanted to be David Hasselhoff, but I sympathized with him. All he wanted was his freedom, but the price of living without any responsibilities usually comes with an irreparable mistake, one that each and every human makes, sooner or later, to come out stronger on the other side.

The Wizened Ex-Playboy Goes Sexual Predator After Indulging Every Affordable Vice

I saw people on the street dressed for winter, in toques and mitts and winter coats. There was a commotion in a nearby alley, and I saw Mike "The Situation" appear out from behind a dumpster. He was pale and dressed almost all in rags, and a baseball cap. It seemed that he had attempted to assault an elderly woman, who sprayed him in the eyes with pepper spray.

He hid in a cardboard box while the woman tried to flag down a police officer passing through the intersection. The police officer ignored the woman, so I decided to walk across the street and deal with "The Situation" myself.

I kicked his cardboard box. Mike "The Situation" said, "Sorry," in a tone that was obviously lacking in remorse. He told me to, "Lighten up, bro." Then he poked his head out with a goofy smile on his face. Even then I could tell that Mike "The Situation" had much more muscle mass on his body than me, despite being presumably homeless.

Luckily, I was trained in the martial art of Brazilian jiu-jitsu, so when he stepped up to take a swing at me, I was able to subdue him with ease. I put him in a chokehold and made him beg for mercy. I felt guilty for being so ruthless. Then I remembered what Mike "The Situation" had done, or tried to do, to that elderly woman, and wrung his neck harder.

He somehow wiggled out of my grasp and raised his voice to say, "I am an extremely aggressive dude that is ripped up like Rambo, and can jump and kick like Van Damme." He jumped and kicked me in the face, then made a run for it, but fortunately ran right into the chest of another police officer that had just happened to be walking down the block.

The police officer was wearing a pair of glasses that mirrored the sunlight to a blinding degree. The reflection shined right into the eyes of Mike "The Situation", who screamed, "My eyes!" The police officer knocked him to the ground, and stepped on his chest, reading his Miranda rights in a deadpan tone.

I was happy to have helped stop a bad guy but was a bit disturbed when the police officer continually electrocuted him with his stun gun, laughing hysterically after previously showing no emotion whatsoever. After taking my statement, he said, "You did not see anything," and drove Mike "The Situation," who was from then on known in the criminal justice system as Michael Sorrentino, and in his prison block as Lil' Bitch, down to the station. There, they processed the end of what was once the mediocre career of a substandard human being.

Discrimination Is the Latest Trend

At breakfast, Mel Gibson cried into his bowl of bran flakes. I found something endearing about a grown man crying while he ate his cereal. Mel Gibson was upset because I called him an "old man." I only meant that he acted like an old man, not that he was actually an elderly person. I told him that sixty was the new twenty, even though by that math I would not have been born yet.

After a cup of coffee, I treated Mel Gibson to a manicure as compensation for my insensitive statement. He got a paraffin wax treatment from a very hairy man. The very hairy man offered me a buy one get one free deal so that I could have my skin softened as well, but I declined. The very hairy man looked sad after that like he might start crying at any moment.

I told him that I changed my mind, but instead got my nails painted a mango shade by a very happy, very hairy man. When he finished, my fingers looked quite fetching.

Mel Gibson and I decided to go to the nearest Starbucks to show off our freshly groomed hands to the people who were drinking coffee and on their laptops. A bearded guy with glasses aggressively glanced at me with constant eye flicks and no smile. That hurts, I thought. It was inhuman. He was slaying me.

Mel Gibson asked the bearded guy with glasses if he smelled something bad because his facial expression appeared as if he smelled something awful.

It turned out that the bearded guy with glasses was actually a homophobic hipster, who assumed that Mel Gibson and I was a gay couple. "Well, what if we are?" I asked. "This is the twenty-first century." The homophobic hipster took a picture of us with his vintage camera phone and threatened to expose our relationship to a local news source.

Mel Gibson said, "I really cannot have you do that," and took out a stun gun, which he fired into the chest of the homophobic hipster. Then he told me, "That was a close one. I can not have people thinking I am both old and gay."

I was irate! It turned out Mel Gibson was also a homophobic hipster, who was posing as an old man. Then I realized that hipsters had more in common with senior citizens than I had ever previously thought possible. I snatched the vintage camera phone off of the ground, and sent out the picture of us to every contact listed, including TMZ, with the caption, Love at last, free and unfettered. Mel Gibson told me that we were not friends anymore, and I said "Good." Then he shot me with his stun gun.

The Alternate Side

I saw Jerry Seinfeld at a corner store in New York last week. I told him how amazing it was to see him in person, but that I didn't want to be annoying by asking him to take a picture with me. Jerry Seinfeld said, "Oh, the way you are right now?" I was bewildered, and responded "What?" but he kept interrupting me and repeating, "What? What? What?" as he threateningly waved his fist in my face.

I withdrew back into the shampoo aisle and heard him giggle as I crept away. When I went to pay for a bottle of conditioner, I saw Jerry Seinfeld try to stroll out the door with at least twenty bags of pretzels in his arms without paying.

The man behind the counter was very professional, and said, "Excuse me, sir, you still have to pay for those." At first, Jerry Seinfeld pretended to have a hearing disability, but eventually came back to pay for his food. When the man behind the counter took one bag of pretzels and scanned it several times in a row, Jerry Seinfeld stopped him and asked that he scan each pack individually to "avert electrical interference," turning around to wink at me between each beep of the OCR device.

After the man behind the counter had finished scanning each separate pack, he put them into a plastic bag. He began to state the price, but Jerry Seinfeld kept cutting him short by yawning obnoxiously. Then he said, "Sometimes the road less traveled is less traveled for a reason," and walked out of the store empty-handed, calling back inside at the last second to say, "Thanks anyhow, for nothing, though."

Attack of the Offensively Insipid, Unfunny, Infantile, Slapstick Man-Children

I was trying to teach Adam Sandler salsa dancing for his thirteen-year anniversary with his wife, Jackie Sandler. Admittedly, Adam Sandler's face instinctually made me angry, which caused me to become impatient with him whenever he missed a step. With each mistake he made, Adam Sandler's visible frustration grew. The laugh lines he'd gained from phony movie guffaws turned into frown lines that looked like scratches around his thin lips.

My breaking point came when Adam Sandler stepped on my foot. I swore he did it on purpose, so I stepped on his foot back. There we were, two grown men, trying to step on each other's feet as hard as we could. That was when I realized that Adam Sandler had been wearing open toe sandals the entire time that we were dancing. I was about to tell him that this was an easy problem to solve when he did a two-finger whistle to signal for backup.

Kevin James entered the studio wearing steel-toed Kodiak work boots. I did not want to have my toes broken by Kevin James' crushing bulk, so I fled toward the door but was cut off by a katana-wielding Rob Schneider. I used a Krav Maga evasive maneuver that I'd learned in a YMCA self-defense class to disarm Rob Schneider with ease, and held the katana to his throat. Adam Sandler got down on his knees and began to whine for mercy.

I told him that if he gave me the remote control prop from the movie Click, we could call it even. Adam Sandler, who I knew kept the remote control prop on his person at all times, agreed and handed it over begrudgingly. "Nice doing business with you boys," I said in a grating, gimmicky, high-pitched tone, and made a dramatic exit even though I had another lesson to give David Spade at the top of the hour.

I'll Go Crazy If I Don't Go Crazy Tonight

Bono built bombs in his basement in preparation for the apocalypse. He said that whether it was virus-ridden toads falling from the sky or zombies climbing out of graves, he would be ready. He had a stack of metal pipes, fuel containers, and propane that he'd stolen from Sears during their Labor Day sale. The store didn't have enough security to stop people from looting, and he was able to sneak in and out without being detected.

I told Bono that what he'd done was not only illegal but also creepy. He pulled down his fly sunglasses so that I could see his eyes. His sunglasses slid in front of a fluorescent ceiling light, casting an eerie, segmented shadow across the room. He fidgeted with the frames, which made for a bouncing illusion that was hypnotic.

Bono's eyes were like that of a Basilisk. I was paralyzed and felt my blood turn cold. It was the first time I'd made prolonged eye contact with another human in years, which made me feel incredibly vulnerable. Bono had the ability to read minds, and it felt like my brain was being nursed by hungry kittens, draining every thought I had.

When he finished, Bono said, "Google owns your intellect," and explained what it really meant to live in the world. He told me that I needed to capitulate to the unknown technological overlords that operate the outskirts of society rather than the networks they control. Bono believed that building a computer colossus was the only guaranteed way to protect the Earth from the inevitable apocalypse, and I was starting to think that he was right.

There was a knock on the door during the conversation, and the voice of a woman saying, "This is the police. Come out with your hands up." The knocks grew louder. I wanted to run away, but couldn't escape Bono's gaze. I wasn't sure why he wasn't reacting to the cops breaking down his door. I thought maybe it was because he wanted to get caught. He wanted to save the world, but couldn't offer any real solutions.

Jodie Foster entered the house and tackled Bono to the floor. She strapped a wire cage to his face, and a leather strap over his eyes so that he couldn't bite or entrance anyone. I acted as if I were a hostage even though I was there by my own volition, and Jodie Foster told me that I could take one thing from Bono's house as recompense before being set free.

At first, I went for his fly sunglasses, but Jodie Foster stopped me. "He has glaucoma," she said, and I instantly felt guilty. I decided to take the second best thing, his honorary knighthood. I'd earned it by defending the world from a potential terror threat. There was no telling where those bombs were going to end up, but my guess was that they wouldn't be put to use against virus-ridden toads falling from the sky or zombies climbing out of graves. The apocalypse would not be for years, and bombs would not be necessary. There would be plenty of time to build a computer colossus before then.

The Dark Night Rises Before the Dawn of Justice

I was taking espresso shots with Christian Bale and Ben Affleck after the premiere of the new Catwoman movie, starring Halle Berry. Ben Affleck and Christian Bale's conversation consisted of remarks on how foxy Catwoman was, and how they were both super jealous that Idris Elba was playing Batman, though they acknowledged that he was more handsome than either of them.

After their sixth cup of coffee each, Christian Bale and Ben Affleck simultaneously excused themselves to use the bathroom. I decided to go in after them after a half hour had passed and found Ben Affleck face down on a toilet seat sniffing cocaine with a rolled up hundred dollar bill. Christian Bale was looking at himself in the mirror and laughing maniacally, repeating the word "Cabbagetown," over and over. Cabbagetown was the name of the gentlemen's club where Christian Bale and Ben Affleck were members.

I volunteered to be designated driver for the sake of their safety and tried to stay calm as Christian Bale stuck his head out of my sun roof screaming obscenities while Ben Affleck wept softly in the back seat. Each time I looked in my rearview mirror, Ben Affleck's face was alternating between smiles and cries. It was insanely creepy.

When we arrived at Cabbagetown, Christian Bale showed his card to the bouncer at the door. The bouncer told Christian Bale that he was banned after the last time when he tried to bring a chainsaw into the club. Ben Affleck had no problem getting in, and I followed him to get away from Christian Bale, who left to hitchhike down the highway. Interestingly enough, the driver who picked him up was never seen again.

Ben Affleck offered to buy me a lap dance, but I told him that I was just going to have some food at the buffet. There was lobster ravioli, macaroni and bacon bits, fried turkey, pita bread, rice and black beans pilaf, and an inexplicable gallon-sized jug of mayonnaise, which I put on everything. I only got to go one round on the buffet, though, because Ben Affleck was kicked out for repeatedly trying to climb on stage and take his clothes off, while crying, and periodically laughing.

I drove him back to my apartment and said that he could sleep on my couch, though I didn't entirely trust him. I took a shower and got ready to sleep. I turned off the light and crawled into bed, pulled the covers over my head and shut my eyes. Then I heard it, the sound of soft panting coming from underneath the mattress. I opened my eyes to see a set of red pupils gleaming from the floor. It was the psychopathic gaze of Christian Bale, who'd broken into my apartment and hidden under my bed while we were at Cabbagetown.

I reached over to the nightstand and grabbed my copied color reproduction of the complete script for The Karate Kid, signed by Pat Morita and Ralph Macchio. I swung for the red eyes with the script and heard a slapping sound. I called for Ben Affleck's assistance. He came running in with a couch cushion, which he swung slumber party style at Christian Bale, knocking him unconscious. I thanked Ben Affleck for saving my life and asked him what we should do with Christian Bale. Ben Affleck replied, "If I ever woke up with a dead hooker in my hotel room, Matt Damon would be the first person I'd call." I was disturbed by this response and decided to call some friends I had in law enforcement: David Duchovny and Gillian Anderson.

They showed up within five minutes of my call, completely drenched despite the fact that it was not raining outside. Gillian Anderson handcuffed Christian Bale while David Duchovny read him his rights. Christian Bale started to stir and to look up to the ceiling. Then he spoke in some foreign tongue that none of us could recognize. There was a flash of light and David Duchovny screamed, "Unidentified flying object at twelve o'clock!" I looked to my right, my left, and then I saw it, some sort of spacecraft with a beam shining down on Christian Bale. There was another flash, and then he was gone, vanished into nothingness.

David Duchovny dropped to his knees and screamed,"Noooooooooooo!" knowing that this was the closest he'd ever been to an alien, and he'd missed his opportunity to interact with them. Ben Affleck was crying on the floor out of fear, and Gillian Anderson was watching both of them, shaking her head. I told them all that I was exhausted, and had to wake up early the next morning for work. In the end, I only got two hours of sleep, but my job was at Starbucks, so I had some hair of the dog in the form of espresso shots. In some ways, the combination of high caffeine, low energy made me feel like I was starting to go insane. It was a feeling that I enjoyed.

"There is always some madness in love. But there is also always some reason in madness."

— Friedrich Nietzsche

An Illegitimate Sponsorship for Someone Incapable of Independent Thought

I moved into a house with John Stamos, Bob Saget, and Dave Coulier so that the three of them could help me end my coffee addiction. I'd been drinking espresso with every meal for the past five years, and couldn't handle the withdrawal on my own. I was eating more food so that I could drink coffee without getting such intense heart palpitations. I didn't think that things could get any worse. I was wrong.

John Stamos, Bob Saget, and Dave Coulier each turned out to be an addict as well. John Stamos was a sex addict and had a different man or woman over each hour of every day to hump. He'd been doing it ever since the media exposed his toupee, causing him to abandon his rock star ambitions for meaningless intercourse. Bob Saget was a porn addict but said that he would have been a sex addict like John Stamos if anyone on Earth found him remotely attractive. Dave Coulier was addicted to helium because of the funny voices that he could make while inhaling it. He'd huffed so much helium that his head was beginning to disintegrate.

The three of them kept hypocritically saying that I needed to drink less coffee, but whenever my buzz wore off I would feel like I was dying. I knew that they were just trying to help and that I'd asked for it, but nothing that any of them said seemed remotely beneficial. I decided to seek out the only other person who I knew that had openly struggled with addiction: Mary-Kate Olsen.

When I found her, she was wearing a fifty-five thousand dollar Nile crocodile skin backpack studded with prescription pills. It was a beautiful piece of art, and I contemplated selling my soul to get my hands on one. Mary-Kate Olsen said that instead, she would give me her backpack if I agreed to give up coffee for good. I accepted her offer and wore that backpack every day for the rest of my life. It was my most expensive possession, and I wanted to make others feel inferior for not having an equally extravagant product. I had no idea that Mary-Kate Olsen's backpack was actually embossed cowhide that had a fishy, swampy, salty smell by coincidence. I was fine not knowing.

Bystanders Subjected to the Threat of Violence Are Not Always Subject to Fear (and Vice Versa)

I was waiting in line at the bank when I noticed Macaulay Culkin standing behind me. I happened to have tickets to see his cover band The Pizza Underground that evening at an abandoned warehouse by the pier and started asking him questions like if there would be any kazoo solos at the show. Macaulay Culkin responded, "Only kazoo solos." While we talked, Joe Pesci popped out from behind a plant with a shotgun in his hand. He told us to relinquish our wallets if we wanted to live.

Macaulay Culkin had a crazy look on his face, and I could tell that he was plotting something devious. Joe Pesci said that if we didn't do what he said, he would "bite off every one of our little fingers, one at a time." Then Joe Pesci turned to me and said, "I'll snap off your cajones and boil them in motor oil."

A police officer that had been smoking a cigarette outside came into the bank and told Joe Pesci to freeze. While he was distracted, Macaulay Culkin took a slice of pizza out of his pocket and threw it in the face of Joe Pesci. The grease got into his eyes, and Joe Pesci began to shoot wildly in all directions. Macaulay Culkin dove behind the teller's station and snatched a dye pack, which he tossed like a grenade at the feet of Joe Pesci. The dye pack released aerosol and tear gas in short blinding bursts.

Joe Pesci screamed out in pain and dropped his shotgun, but Macaulay Culkin wasn't finished with him yet. He pulled a suspicious roll of duct tape from his back pocket and wrapped Joe Pesci up like a Christmas present. Then he went out to his car to "get his blowtorch and pliers." As soon as he left, though, the police officer locked the doors to keep Macaulay Culkin out, and Joe Pesci inside.

I hid in the bank's vault until backup arrived and arrested both Macaulay Culkin and Joe Pesci, who each already had warrants out for their arrests for multiple home invasions and kidnapping.

When I got back to my apartment, the first thing that I did was take a shower. I wanted to wash the feeling of the day off of me and get ready for the night. Then I realized that Macaulay Culkin wouldn't be able to perform with The Pizza Underground because he was in prison, so there would be no concert. I decided that the best alternative would be to order a large supreme pizza to eat alone in my dark bedroom, watching Munchies on YouTube so that I didn't feel so isolated.

In the end, I decided to focus my childlike enthusiasm on rigging the apartment with booby traps, mostly to distract from my loneliness, but also just in case of a burglary. It was a win-win scenario.

Good Things Can Happen When You Move out of Your Comfort Zone

I saw a man meandering across the street and knew his face from having been plastered across the walls of my sister's room when she was a teenager. When he came closer, I recognized him as a much older, more unkempt Jonathan Taylor Thomas. I asked him where he was going, and he told me where he had been.

I was shocked to find out that Jonathan Taylor Thomas was the voice of Simba in the Lion King. I suggested that he get back into voice-over acting. Jonathan Taylor Thomas said, "Puberty was a bitch," and I realized that he no longer had the capacity to speak with the resplendence required of a cute cartoon character.

He asked if I would help him steal batteries from a nearby convenience store. There was a police car in the parking lot, but Jonathan Taylor Thomas told me not to worry. Then he randomly stated that some prisons were cool for allowing their inmates to wear jeans. I said that there was nothing cool about prison.

The convenience store was empty aside from a cashier, who was the tallest woman I had ever seen. She could crane her line of vision into any aisle, and eyed us with suspicion as we huddled around the electronics section.

Jonathan Taylor Thomas pocketed packs of D batteries and told me to grab something useful. I stuffed a flashlight down my pant leg and positioned a calculator in my waistband. As we walked toward the exit, the cashier pulled a gun out from under the counter and aimed it at us.

I knew that we were in danger of being killed at any moment. Jonathan Taylor Thomas tried and failed to charm the cashier with his manly voice. The cashier told us to strip off our clothes. I thought Maybe Jonathan Taylor Thomas was more charming than I initially thought.

Once we were naked, the cashier took back the goods that we had hidden, and then pointed at the exit. I asked her if we could have our clothes back, and she pointed the gun directly at me. Once we were outside, the police officer exited his vehicle and told us to stop where we were. He asked where our clothes had gone. I said, "The cashier took them." Jonathan Taylor Thomas asked the police officer, "What are you going to do about it?"

The police officer chased us naked down the street, and I must say, despite the loss of his cute cartoon character voice, I was jealous of Jonathan Taylor Thomas' devil-may-care attitude, and his hair, which even after an evening in jail, did not lose its luster.

If You Stand for Nothing, You'll Fall for Anything (Originality)

After hanging out on house arrest with Gucci Mane, I was inspired to get a face tattoo of my own. I wanted it to be food-related like Gucci Mane's ice cream cone, but something salty instead of sweet. Justin Bieber wanted to get a face tattoo to match mine, so I told him we could each get a variation on a classic: the potato chip.

I wanted my potato chip to be a light shade of green like the potato hadn't quite ripened before being processed. Justin wanted his darker, and more kettle cooked in appearance. We went to see Kat Von D for our tattoos. I was so excited. My soul started shaking like it was freezing to death.

When we got there, it turned out that there was a wait. Soulja Boy had come straight from the airport and was already getting his face tattooed before his concert that night. Justin Bieber decided to change his mind at the last second, to get a little cross on his cheek like Soulja Boy instead of the original potato chip idea, which was an eye-opening moment for me. I realized then that Justin Bieber wasn't a trendsetter at all. He was a follower, a loyal disciple to the industry gods.

Justin Bieber admitted that he was scared of the hummingbird-sized needle piercing his luscious face skin. I told him to bury everything that he thought so that his mind would be a blank slate that couldn't comprehend discomfort. Justin Bieber cleared his head of all thoughts and kept a straight face as Kat Von D dug the needle deep into his eyelid tissue.

When she finished, Justin Bieber looked infinitely more badass. He smiled big, showing his platinum grill. I asked him if it hurt as bad as he expected, and Justin Bieber looked back at me with an expressionless stare, as if the words I said made little to no sense. I suspected that he temporarily forgot how to speak, and confirmed this theory when Kat Von D asked Justin Bieber if he liked his new tattoo, and Justin Bieber responded with a fit of giggles.

Then it was my turn. I decided to change my mind at the last second too. I was going to do something different, and get something entirely new. I was going to shave my head, and get five different red star tattoos on the various sides of my skull. First, Soulja Boy did the honors of cutting my hair with a razor that he had in his traveling bag. I tried to project a cheerful image as I watched my hair fall to the floor around my feet, instantly regretting the choice that I'd made, but knowing that it was too late to go back.

Kat Von D stuck her needle into my temple, and that is the last thing I remembered. My body went into shock from a single pinprick, and when I woke up, there were TMZ cameras all around. I tried so hard to get away, but no one would let me through. I fell to the floor and covered my face with my hands like the cover artwork to Fetty Wap's eponymous debut album. Justin Bieber was gone, and I felt incredibly alone, curled up in a ball on the floor of High Voltage Tattoo Parlor, breathing in and out at a peculiar rhythm that only served to increase my anxiety.

That's when I heard the song over the shop speakers: First Day Out tha Feds by Gucci Mane. I heard him say "But I bend don't break, I don't ask just take, black gloves, black tape and I don't play nor pray. Wake up and take a piss, I hear em sharpening knives, main focus every day is make it out here alive."

I was motivated by the defiant words of the realist trap god and fought through the camera flashes and blinking lights with every last bit of energy I had. Mike Will Made It's layered synthesizers propelled me forward until I was out of the shop, and back on the street in West Hollywood.

A minute later I hopped in an Uber and told the driver to take me anywhere. As we drove away, I saw Justin Bieber standing alone on the sidewalk, unsure what to do since he had nobody to imitate. The last thing that I saw was Justin Bieber being tackled and pummeled by paparazzi. I felt sorry and not sorry, and after stopping off for ice cream and potato chips on the way home, I felt nothing at all.

Golf is a White-Knuckle Ride of Emotional and Physical Duress

By the time I made it onto the green, Frankie Muniz was ahead of me by a single stroke. With twenty feet between himself and the hole, Frankie Muniz pulled back his putter, then swung it forward. The wind blew the ball wide, and I pumped my fist in celebration. Frankie Muniz grimaced at me. It was a tie, and if he missed the next putt, the game would likely be mine. After taking a deep breath, shaking out his arms, aiming his clubface, and aligning his shoulders, he finally took the shot.

At first, I thought he had hit the ball too hard, and yelled, "I win!" It turned out to be a better shot than I thought, and the ball, seeming to curve ninety degrees at the last second, went into the hole. Frankie Muniz gave me the middle finger, then pulled on his putter as if it was his penis, and he was masturbating in my direction. It was a tasteless move, and the spectators began to boo.

The commissioner of the golf tournament disqualified Frankie Muniz for unsportsmanlike conduct and said that in the process of beating him, I had set a new course record. I told the commissioner that I did not want to win by disqualification, and suggested that Frankie Muniz should face me in a cage match to determine the winner of the tournament.

The commissioner led us to a steel cage just beyond the eighteenth hole, with blood and sweat stains on the canvas. Frankie Muniz and I agreed to use our caddies as our corner men for the fight. My caddy was Michael B. Jordan, and Frankie Muniz' caddie was Miles Teller, which reinforced my confidence because I believed that Michael B. Jordan could probably beat Miles Teller in a fight if he wanted to.

Frankie Muniz and I agreed to a no-holds-barred match where each of us could use a golf club as a weapon. I initially chose my driver, but Michael B. Jordan suggested I go with the pitching wedge instead. Frankie Muniz informed me that he'd bought his set of titanium golf clubs at a police auction, and chose the 5-iron because that particular club was once involved in a violent murder.

Before the fight, the commissioner brought us to the center of the cage and told us to shake hands. I stuck my hand out, and Frankie Muniz slapped it away, saying, "Let's go already!" The fight lasted one round. It began with a swift head-butt from Frankie Muniz. Dazed, I fell back into the cage and received several quick blows to my shins from the 5-iron. I blindly crept across the canvas, then felt the 5-iron's crippling blow to my ribs. It made a terrible cracking sound.

For a moment, I honestly thought Frankie Muniz might kill me, and said a prayer asking God to forgive me for all of my past sins and transgressions. I braced for impact, anticipating darkness at any second as Frankie Muniz raised his club over my head and asked in a villainous tone, "Any last words?"

Then I heard it, a sound of anguish followed by Frankie Muniz's sputtering surrender as my trusty caddy Michael B. Jordan ambushed him from behind, securing a brutal figure-four leglock that the commissioner said was entirely legal in a no-holds-barred match. With the realization that I'd almost died for a sport that I did not care about, I told Frankie Muniz that I was willing to consider the match a draw so that we could let bygones be bygones.

The last straw was when Frankie Muniz held out his hand as if he were finally ready to make amends, just so that I would come close enough for him to spit in my face. I clubbed him in the groin with his 5-iron before the commissioner raised my arm, the new, undisputed champion of the world.

Every Moment Feels like an Altered State

I got lost in a deeply suburban community. It was quite beige, aside from the grass that was all green, and the street that was black. There were no yellow lines to separate the lanes, which proved especially confusing for Zach Braff, who had just moved into a house at the end of the cul-de-sac after returning from a year in Manchester for the filming of a new romantic comedy about depression. I asked him how his trip went, and he said, "Yeah, pretty well."

He invited me over for a housewarming party, which consisted of just the two of us. We ingested some ecstasy in his unfurnished basement. He offered me a beer, and I asked whether or not alcohol was good to mix with other drugs. Zach Braff said that one drink "obviously" would not make a difference. I said, "Cool. In that case, I will take a lite." I felt drunk after only one beer and thought that maybe Zach Braff had tricked me when he said that one drink "obviously" would not make a difference.

There was a long pause as we both considered what to do for fun. I stated that we should invite over intelligent, and introspective women to talk about life, while on ecstasy. Zach Braff said that he knew a ton of chicks. Then he spent over an hour looking through his contacts, stating something vaguely wrong with each woman whose name he came across, besides his mom, which I thought was strange. In a joking tone, I said, "You should tell your mom to come party with us."

A few minutes later Zach Braff's mom arrived, appearing as if she had already done drugs by the way her eyes refused to focus on one point for more than a second or two. Before I even got the chance to introduce myself, Zach Braff's mom said, "Let's get fucked up," and placed a big bag of cocaine on the table. Zach Braff asked, "What are you doing, mom?" She told him in a gentle way that his father had been dead for over ten years, and that she had recently begun dating a new man by the name of Sebastian, who was a wonderful human being, and the primary cocaine distributor for the Tri-County area. Zach Braff's voice cracked as he shrilly repeated, "What are you doing, mom?"

I felt immense discomfort socially but was relaxed physically due to the effects of the ecstasy in my system. I felt how I imagined Zach Braff's character in Garden State must have felt when he ingested ecstasy at his friend's party, yet remained detached from everything and everyone around him, with the world moving past, and blurring into formlessness. The difference was that Zach Braff's character smoked marijuana in that scene. I had not smoked any marijuana in Zach Braff's basement.

I stood up, and Zach Braff's mom stared directly at me. I said, "I am going to find marijuana." Zach Braff's mom smiled and said, "I have some right here for you, Hun." Then she explained that Sebastian was also a harvester of marijuana and that she had been encouraging him to expand his business for some time. "He is such a talented person," she kept saying. For a third time, Zach Braff asked, "What are you doing, mom," to which she replied, "I am sorry, Hun. Both of my men are talented people."

The atmosphere seemed to mellow after we smoked a couple of joints. I felt myself drifting toward sleep right as Zach Braff said, "I just want what is best for you." I dreamt that Sebastian came over to the house, and imagined him as a tall, olive-skinned Adonis with a ponytail that hung past his shoulders. Zach Braff and Sebastian promptly became best friends and snorted cocaine together until the sun came up, while Zach Braff's mom watched, filled with joy from drugs, and because she had both of her favorite people under the same roof for the first time in ten years.

"Optimism is the madness of insisting that all is well when we are miserable."

— Voltaire

Capturing Sensory-Overloaded Hyper-Presence (Transcendence)

A pamphlet listed the best places to cry on campus. I had trouble deciding between the coffee shop and the computer lab. I did not want to cry into a keyboard by accident, so I chose the coffee shop. There was no coffee, and the shop was actually an underground tunnel.

It contained a series of booths with curtains, behind which was sobbing. I thought I recognized a few people by the way they heaved their breath and sighed between shudders. My suspicions were confirmed when James Franco appeared out from one of the booths with tears in his eyes. He said that he was crying on cue for practice and that he was not actually depressed, or anything like that. He said that crying had gotten him out of trouble in the past. "Big trouble with bad people." James Franco invited me back to his apartment for a free lesson in crying on cue.

I sat on his couch and waited as he disappeared down a small hallway where I assumed his bedroom was, calling out, "Take your shirt off." I asked him why that was necessary. He told me that crying on cue was a logical progression, and the first step was for me to let myself become vulnerable. When he reappeared, I asked James Franco why he had a camera, and why he was taking pictures of me with my shirt off. He said that it was all a part of the process.

There was a knock at the door, and James Franco told me to hide. Seth Rogan entered, and seeing me shirtless said, "What the heck dude?" I said, "This is weird," then put my shirt back on, and ran out the door. James Franco's voice echoed, "This is all part of the process."

Following the strange encounter, I decided to go to the computer lab. There were no computers, and the lab was actually a theater, with a balcony overlooking the stage. I thought about what James Franco said about letting myself become vulnerable, and walked to the front and center. As students slowly turned their heads up to watch me, I began to move, breathe and let out the sounds I would usually have made if I were genuinely crying.

Then my eyes slowly swelled as I sensually re-created the circumstances leading up to the event. I cried in front of everyone, and everyone was crying. Tears flowed at the top of the hour when the students had to leave for their next classes. They gradually cleared out until there was nobody left, except me, in the spotlight, and one other person. I squinted and saw through my misty eyes that it was James Franco, pointing at me from the balcony, with a camera.

Filling the Void of a Gaping Emotional Black Hole

Chad Michael Murray looked at himself in the mirror for a year straight after growing attached to his reflection, the one friend who never left him. I told him that he was not alone. I too had abandonment issues. Chad Michael Murray pressed his palm to the mirror and said, "A perfect match."

I told him that staying glued to his reflection all day was unhealthy and that he needed sunlight and exercise, or else he would wither away. Chad Michael Murray said, "I will never leave this room again, not even to use the bathroom." I thought, "Oh shit. He is worse than I expected." I did not want to enable his reclusive behavior and stopped the supply of food, multi-vitamins, and toilet paper that I had previously felt compelled to bring by his room once a week.

A month later I decided to surprise Chad Michael Murray with a bacon cheeseburger, which was his favorite food, though he had only ever eaten three in his entire life because of their unhealthy ingredients and unnecessarily high caloric total. When I found him, he was staring at himself in the mirror and repeatedly muttering, "Flawless," in regards to his body, which had lost nearly half of its mass. I realized that the only way to save Chad Michael Murray was to break the mirror. Otherwise, there was no telling if he would ever leave the house again.

I took the Teen Choice Award that was gathering dust on his dresser and hurled it at his reflection. Chad Michael Murray collapsed along with the aluminum glass, saying, "I am alone again. I am alone again. I am alone again," over and over, like an action figure that had its electronic voice box damaged by a manic child repeatedly slamming its body into the ground, over and over, until the crippled action figure could only speak a single, repeating phrase. Luckily, I came prepared with a backup plan. The backup plan was a Komodo dragon.

The particular Komodo dragon had a keen sense for emotional neediness, and upon seeing Chad Michael Murray immediately elongated its neck and posed like a dog that expected to be petted. Chad Michael Murray reached his hand out, and after only a second of contact wailed, "I love him!" He said that owning a Komodo dragon was even better than having a human baby because it did not cry or vomit. I saw the same affection glowing in his eyes for the Komodo dragon that he had for himself when he looked in the mirror, forming like an invisible attachment that grew stronger with each moment they spent together.

Chad Michael Murray thanked me for saving his life in a tone that seemed both grateful and abrupt, as if he was appreciative, but also wanted some time alone with his newfound soul mate. Then, on my way out of the door, he said, "Wait, I almost forgot," and took the bacon cheeseburger out of my hand. I was happy to see that nature had once again regained its course.

The Complex Lifestyle of a Loner (Facelove)

I passed Tony Hawk grinding outside of Starbucks. He was wearing incredibly stylish socks with skulls on the sides. My camouflage parka blended in with my surroundings. I was in a perpetual struggle to detach the camouflage parka from my soul. My phone warned me that I would go deaf if the volume got any higher. I raised even more sound. There was an anticlimax when I tried to play the song Sk8er Boi by Avril Lavigne for Tony Hawk. I must have played the instrumental version by accident.

As I sharply turned the corner while comically puffing my cheeks out and exhaling, I ended up gently blowing into the face of Tony Hawk, who was walking in the opposite direction. He gave me a playful push before we engaged in social interaction, trading cheekbone compliments for jawline praise.

I told him that the scar tissue on his chin was beautiful, iridescent, and pearl-like. He said that I had the taut face of a wooden puppet. We shared the word successful until I took the word success and he took the word rich. The next step in this cosmic development would be to become best friends, but seclusion with no external contact was how I succeeded in this world. I continued toward my destination of the Starbucks bathroom, to bathe and stuff paper towels into a hand dryer that I mistook for a trash bin.

Mortality, the Passing of Time, and the Problem of Loneliness

I posted an ad in the strictly platonic section of Craigslist after spending over a week alone in my apartment and smoking three bowls of marijuana. The title of the ad was *I Am Really Lonely*. After sorting through several replies that consisted mostly of penis pictures, I received a positive response from somebody looking to hang out. Her name was Emma Watson.

She wrote in her initial email that frequently traveling made it hard for her to create real connections with other human beings. I told her that I could relate. After a month of messaging back and forth, we met at the Macaroni Grill, where the tablecloths were construction paper, and the waiters brought crayons to draw on the tablecloth.

It gave me a break from sleeping, and her from the filming of a new Harry Potter prequel. I asked if the movie would take place before or after Harry Potter's parents were killed by the alien invasion. She asked if I had ever even read the books. I read the first book once while I was simultaneously on mushrooms and watching the X-Files, but told Emma Watson that I had not read any of the Harry Potter books.

Having taken a look at her Twitter account before our meet up, I saw that Emma Watson posted a harsh article condemning psychedelics as a high-risk, low-reward effort employed by the creatively uninspired, which I thought was inaccurate when I considered my experience. I wanted to prove to her that psychedelics were actually a low-risk, high-reward means to enlightenment.

I excused myself from the table so that I could take a tab of acid in the bathroom. When I returned, Emma Watson had already finished her second glass of wine and was waving her hand to get the waiter's attention like an overenthusiastic student who had the answer to the teacher's question, and could only just barely keep from calling out before the teacher acknowledged them.

I noticed that she had drawn a picture on the tablecloth of a little girl, with a face that was expressionless, sitting under a tree in what was either rain or falling leaves. It was hard to tell. By the time the acid kicked in,

Emma Watson looked like a two-dimensional geometric octopus, waving her tentacles in every direction. I told her that she was quite beautiful for a cephalopod. She said, "Thank you," in a tone that was underhandedly sarcastic, and for the rest of dinner, which was just breadsticks, stared at me the way somebody who condemned psychedelics might look at a person who they suspected had snuck off to ingest drugs, more specifically, psychedelics.

Finally, I decided enough was enough and picked up one of the crayons. I wrote, "I do not want you to be lonely," next to the little girl that Emma Watson had drawn. Then I took my best shot at sketching a stick figure friend for the little girl, which despite its ill proportions, made Emma Watson smile for the first time that evening.

Her appearance changed from that of a two-dimensional geometric octopus into a three-dimensional isometric peacock. She was much more colorful and said "Thank you," in a tone that was sincere, looking at me the way somebody who had just made a real connection might gaze at the person with whom they had just made that connection.

Emma Watson said, "I think that I am finally ready to try some psychedelics." I gave her a handful of mushrooms, and she surprisingly loved the taste. We spent the rest of the night drawing a town on the tablecloth for our doodles to live in, until around eleven o'clock, which was when the Macaroni Grill closed.

Emma Watson told me that we would meet again soon and then skipped away toward the train station several blocks South. I waited on the corner for a bus going North, which left me feeling more sad than usual as I watched the headlights approach like shooting stars, shining down on somebody who was on their way to be alone again.

Trying to Be Capable of Forming True and Meaningful Human Connections

I got trapped in the library after closing time. I thought that the library would be a good place to go if I was ever in need of shelter. It was warm and had plenty of pleasurable reading material. I heard the sound of footsteps, and I hid behind a pile of books. Those footsteps belonged to Meryl Streep. Her badge said, "Librarian." She looked like a librarian, four-eyed and statuesque. Her body cast a shadow in the shape of a honey badger.

The honey badger crept along shelves, sniffing the spines of several poetry collections before arriving in the non-fiction section, where I was sitting in the corner. Meryl Streep told me, "The library is closed," in a tone that sounded as if she was merely fulfilling an obligation to inform me of the policy regarding visiting hours, but did not care that I was breaking the rules. Then she told me that there was coffee on the second floor if I wanted some. I told her that would be nice.

There was a label on the coffee that said decaf. When I asked Meryl Streep if there was anything stronger, she pulled out a bottle of wine from under the table. I asked, "What else do you have hidden under there?"

Meryl Streep revealed three handguns, a knife, Percocet, beer, and an ounce of marijuana, all duct taped to the bottom of the table. She uncorked the wine with the precision of a waitress at a five-star French restaurant. I could tell that both the library and Meryl Streep had more to them than what appeared on the outside, and felt bad for judging them by their exteriors. Likewise, I thought, I would not want her to judge me by my beard and face tattoos.

She asked me if I wanted to go outside to smoke, and I said "Sure." Meryl Streep led me into an alleyway between the library and the café next door. I thought that for all of her excellent qualities, Meryl Streep's one flaw was that she held her cigarette like a European Nazi in a foreign film.

When I corrected her form, she asked, "Does it matter?" I stared at her hand for a moment, then answered, "No, not really."

I decided to leave from there and thanked Meryl Streep for not being one of those librarians that looked down on people for ingesting Adderall or smoking weed before going to the library, to read while peaking, before crashing on the floor, as was my scenario that evening. She told me that most librarians were on drugs, and with a wink, handed me the bottle of wine to finish on my walk.

Complications of Being a Stable Person Who People Expect to Own Certain Items and Dress Certain Ways (An Ever-Darkening Worldview)

After graduating from college, I needed to find a job. But first, I needed to look professional. Anne Hathaway told me about a great deal she could get me on a suit. She took me to a warehouse that appeared to be for importing coffee beans. Anne Hathaway seemed furious, and stomped around saying, "There's supposed to be suits! I do not see any suits!" I told her to take a chill pill, and handed her a Xanax.

After a bit more searching, we found the suit store directly next to a coffee warehouse. It had every kind of suit imaginable, from leather to cashmere, which was upsetting to me as an animal rights advocate because I had recently found out that cashmere came from the hair of goats. The goats lived on farms where farmers dehorned, castrated, and forced them to have their ears notched without anesthesia, which in culmination, gave me a very nauseous feeling in my stomach. I told Anne Hathaway that I did not feel comfortable buying clothes from a store that sold cashmere.

She asked me if I was "mental." I said "Huh?" as if I had not heard her, though I had; I simply had not understood the implication. She asked me if I was "crazy" instead. I said, "Insane in the membrane!" The clerk at the suit store had his eye on me like he thought I was going to walk out wearing one of the suits without paying. Anne Hathaway was doing the opposite of the clerk, looking away from me with the knowledge that I wanted no part in any exchange of capital with a store that sold cashmere.

She said, "We can try someplace else," in a tone that showed her lack of faith in finding a clothing store that did not sell a single cashmere item. Then she said, "Let's go," like she wanted to leave just so that she could have one of those "I told you so," moments when our mission proved impossible. I told her that I was tired and that maybe we should try another time. She asked, "What other time? This is it!" I said, "No thanks then," and went back to my dorm room to smoke some marijuana. I wanted to compound the pain of wasting my time as an adult, by romanticizing the wasted time of my youth.

A Disparate Range of Behaviors (I Want Pure Energy)

When we were young, Kevin Spacey and I would buy a forty-ounce Super Big Gulp from 7-Eleven to make swamp water. We called it 'swamp water', but I've heard others call it a graveyard, zombie, and suicide. To make swamp water, we would pour a little of every beverage into the forty-ounce Super Big Gulp, from Mountain Dew to Dr. Pepper, lemonade to seltzer. Next, we would stir until the concoction was cola-colored. Then we would take turns slurping with straws the size of our forearms until there was no swamp water left.

We pretended that the drink gave us superpowers when really it induced a sugar rush that lasted until bedtime. Kevin Spacey's mom kept a spare pair of scissors on her because each time we drank swamp water, Kevin Spacey would end up with bubblegum stuck in his hair. Kevin Spacey's mom had to cut chunks out of his bowl cut until he had more of a textured punk-style hairdo. I reacted to the sugar by spinning around in circles until I was dizzy, eventually falling to the floor and watching the ceiling spin overhead. It was a magical sensation that I couldn't find anywhere else.

Kevin Spacey and I still make swamp water, but these days we make it out of coffee instead of high fructose corn syrup and sugar water. Yesterday we used every single roast, from hazelnut to French vanilla, pumpkin spice to amaretto. We mixed the smooth with the mellow and the rich with the savory. The result was a full-bodied blend of aromatic ecstasy. We pretended that the swamp water gave us superpowers when we were actually high on caffeine that lingered until bedtime and beyond. Around three in the morning, Kevin Spacey used clippers instead of scissors to cut the bubblegum out of his hair. He kept a buzz cut since he is set to play Lex Luthor in a live action production of Superman Returns. I thought that Kevin Spacey's resemblance was more akin to a less miserable looking Billy Corgan.

Before I left his house, I spun in circles but couldn't last more than thirty seconds before tripping over myself, knocking over Kevin Spacey's Academy Award for Best Actor as I tried to stay standing. Instead of a magical sensation, I felt a transition of identity and self-confidence that only occurred in early middle-aged individuals. It made me realize that pain and nostalgia mean the same thing. Maybe it was a sign that I should grow up.

"He in his madness prays for storms, and dreams that storms will bring him peace."

— Mikhail Lermontov

Transformers, More than Meets the Eye

I imagined that my body's architecture was doghouse-style. As Optimus Prime, I was sent on a mission to a far off world, away from the other Autobots. I was ordered to engage elite Decepticon monsters in combat. To me, it seemed like a suicide mission. My cat was named Shia LaBeouf. There was a badger the size of a horse in my garden. Shia LaBeouf bravely ran out to chase it off. Then Shia LaBeouf licked himself obsequiously.

I picked him up and accidentally walked through an invisible portal that generated evil doppelgängers of us in the form of Batman and Robin. Batman had to have his legs replaced with those of a clone of himself due to an explosive Decepticon surprise attack. Multiple Robins argued about the ethics of such a procedure. They had a massive telekinesis battle. Batman told Robin that they were not best friends anymore. Batman and I entered a Best Friends Competition, but Shia LaBeouf and Robin won. I was jealous.

That's when evil Batman betrayed me by teaming up with Shia LaBeouf in a catch-and-own competition where cats are released into the woods and then caught by contestants who took them home at the end. I signed up in an attempt to win Shia LaBeouf back. The participants turned out to be highly competitive. A pretentious goth gave me a head-butt when I came too close to his tabby cat.

If I wasn't built out of metal, I might have been concussed. I was a robot. Still, I was crying. I never saw Shia LaBeouf again and did not bother to replace him. I hoped that his new life was better than mine, friendless, lost in space somewhere.

Spice up Your Life One More Time

After the Power Rangers had retired, they looked for a new group of teenagers to take their place. The Spice Girls, Scary, Baby, Ginger, Posh, and Sporty, were the first to volunteer, but they need six people to join. I volunteered, but they said I couldn't join because I wasn't a girl. The Spice Girls picked up Britney Spears as their sixth member, which seemed like an unfair advantage due to her distracting star power. The Backstreet Boys were also trying out to be Power Rangers, so I joined them in the competition to see who was worthy of being the next uniformed team to defend the universe.

As it turned out, there would only be one challenge. It was a walk-off judged by Ben Stiller and Owen Wilson, who were both former runway models themselves. The rules were simple: Use your best judgment on what is appropriate, and stay classy.

The Spice Girls went first. The first round was a simple stroll and turn down the catwalk, which each group nailed. The next round was a deer-like prance on the way down, and a robot-like tango on the way back. The round after that was breakdancing, then handstand walks. Both groups were doing well, and it was hard to tell who was in the lead, until the final round.

Each team was expected to build a moving pyramid out of their team members, which they had to walk down the runway and back without falling. The Spice Girls went first. It was Scary, Sporty, and Baby on the bottom, Ginger and Posh in the middle, and Britney Spears on top. Britney Spears screamed, "Mush!" as she was carried forward and back by the Spice Girls, whipping the air with a cat-o'-nine-tails as the Spice Girls whimpered in fear. Their adrenaline made them move in record time, impressing Ben Stiller and Owen Wilson to the point of a standing ovation.

The Backstreet Boys backed out of the competition after seeing how domineering Britney Spears had become. It was clear that she was meant to be a Power Ranger. They gave her a red skin-tight spandex suit and opaque visor to show that she was now the new leader. The Spice Girls also dressed in color-coded uniforms, Ginger in Pink, Baby in Blue, Sporty in Green, Scary in Yellow, and Posh in Black. It was the perfect combination, a rainbow of girl power glowing brightly. The Backstreet Boys looked like a depressing rain cloud in comparison, and I was happy that the right group won. Quitters had no place protecting the world from devastation. That job was for people committed to spreading positive vibes, with strength and courage and a Wonderbra.

The Final High-Octane Installment of a Successful Speed Racer

I was challenged to come out of retirement for a drag race against Dwayne "The Rock" Johnson. It had been over a decade since my pink Hello Kitty themed Top Fuel dragster had seen street action. In the end, it came down to what the fans wanted. Most of them had forgotten who I was. It was my job to remind them.

On his car, Dwayne "The Rock" Johnson had Samoan tribal symbols painted to match the tattoo on his shoulder. It made me feel self-conscious, but not for long. Once we were on the track, I was only focused on winning.

I remained calm even when Dwayne "The Rock" Johnson started trash talking, saying "The Rock will take you down Know Your Role Boulevard, which is on the corner of Jabroni Drive, and check you directly into the Smackdown Hotel!"

Honestly, I didn't understand how this was a threat. The Smackdown Hotel was a reputable facility, and I needed a place to stay for the night that wasn't overly expensive.

A stoplight in the center of the track flashed red, yellow, green and we were off. Dwayne "The Rock" Johnson took an early lead due to a nitro boost. The German Luftwaffe aircraft used a similar maneuver during WWII by injecting nitrous to gain higher altitude. Luckily, my car was built with the elliptical wings of a British Supermarine Spitfire, which increased my top speed ten-fold, and allowed me to coast to the finish line with ease.

Dwayne "The Rock" Johnson was upset that I'd beaten him by such a wide margin, and demanded a rematch, only this time as a footrace. I declined, and announced my re-retirement from drag racing. My adrenal gland just didn't have the capacity to handle it anymore. Instead, I had Ric Flair fill in for me. He was pumped full of HGH and ready to rumble. Dwayne "The Rock" Johnson begrudgingly accepted, and the race was on again.

Ric Flair was surprising fast for an old man. He got off to a great start, but Dwayne "The Rock" Johnson was willing to do anything to win. He grabbed Ric Flair by his robe, which was a fabric made from the same material as antique-style curtains, covered in approximately a thousand rhinestones, and trimmed with hundreds of flamingo feathers. Dwayne "The Rock" Johnson tried to hold on to the material, but the sequins were cutting up his hands. Ric Flair broke free, and as he did his robe spread out and became wing-like, catching the wind and causing him to fly to the finish line faster than Dwayne "The Rock" Johnson's legs could carry him.

It was truly a momentous upset, and one that even Dwayne "The Rock" Johnson couldn't deny. Ric Flair taunted him with his "Wooo!" shout while boasting that "To be 'The Man', you gotta beat the man!" Dwayne "The Rock" Johnson was crying but gave me a friendly chest bump before saying farewell and driving off into the sunset in his inferiorly designed automobile. It was truly painful to watch.

Planets Orbit, People Are Born to Die

I was studying in Starbucks when a wild Nicolas Cage appeared out from under one of the tables, having been secretly stalking me and also craving coffee. The barista called his name, "A Very Berry Hibiscus Refresher for Nicolas Cage," and handed him his cup, which looked like it was filled with blood. Then the barista asked Nicolas Cage why he had an octopus on a leash. Nicolas Cage told her that he took his octopus, which was named Dionysus, wherever he went to improve his acting.

He came over to where I was sitting and asked if he could have a seat. Then he placed Dionysus down on the table and continued to loom over me with a smile that revealed a set of strawberry-stained teeth. He looked like a vampire, and I started to feel nervous from his presence mixed with the Frappuccino and twenty mg of Adderall I had eaten an hour or so before to finish studying for my physiology exam. I was trying to be mostly sober so that I could get a job after I graduated, weaning off of weed with Adderall and Xanax. But after seeing Nicolas Cage, I decided to quit everything all together, except for maybe coffee, which I needed to go to the gym and wake up in the morning.

Nicolas Cage pointed to my textbook and said that he knew everything there was to know about the human body, and I told him that he was mistaking physiology for anatomy, to which he asked, "What is the difference?" I quoted the best answer on Yahoo Answers, which was ranked four out of five stars, saying, "Anatomy is structure and composition, i.e. histology and cellular differentiation. Physiology is a holistic view of how the mechanisms of those parts interact toward homeostasis." Nicolas Cage appeared visibly exasperated by my response, and said, "I am just pretending to be angry right now. I am a fantastic actor." Dionysus appeared incredibly thirsty, and every time I tried to give him water, Nicolas Cage would say, "He doesn't need your charity. He is also just acting."

I thought that Dionysus might die if he did not get some water soon, so I waited until Nicolas Cage finished talking about an acting technique that he dubbed, "Nouveau Shamanic." I pointed in the opposite direction of Dionysus and said, "Is that a swarm of bees?" Nicolas Cage spun around and screamed, "Not the bees!" I knew that Nicholas Cage had an irrational fear of bees ever since he was stung over fifty times in the face by yellow jackets on the set of The Wicker Man.

I stole Dionysus while he was distracted, and escaped to my motorcycle outside. I held the octopus on my lap as we raced toward the closest body of water, which was, unfortunately, the Jersey shore. When we arrived, I could see down the highway that Nicolas Cage was right behind us, his teeth shining red in the moonlight. I ran as fast as I could through the sand with Dionysus strapped to my chest, and when we reached the water, I leaped forward, through a wave that broke the tentacles' grip, and swept Dionysus away with the tide, back to his family, or so I hoped.

Nicolas Cage opened fire on me with a crossbow from about a hundred feet away and missed by approximately thirty yards. He was a terrible shot, and he knew it. He took a spear out of the trunk of his car and charged toward me with an expression of madness on his face, still smiling, screaming profanity through his clenched teeth. Nicolas Cage tried to stab me unsuccessfully, and then frustrated, tried to tackle me underwater. He was ridiculously uncoordinated, and I wondered if he was on a harder drug than the Very Berry Hibiscus Refresher, like maybe nitrous oxide.

I noticed a fin circling him, and said, "Watch out, that might be a shark!" Nicolas Cage told me I was an idiot, and that it was obviously the dorsal fin of a dolphin. That was when a killer whale sprang from the depths, and in one motion devoured Nicolas Cage whole. I screamed at what I felt was a higher octave than usual, and instinctually ran in reverse toward the shore, a form of retro locomotion that I hoped might rewind time to a point before the killer whale's brutal and indiscriminate slaughter of a man who likely belonged in a mental hospital.

Old World Monkeys

One afternoon in my garden, I decided to catch grasshoppers with a net gun. I tied up a bundle of worms with string so that they would all become Siamese. I had a premonition the night before that an earthquake would hit Japan. In the dream, I was in an elementary school classroom with a Japanese man. He shouted, "Earthquake!" The ground shook, and I fell through the floor. When the aftershock ended, I climbed back up. The man shouted, "Tsunami!" Then a humungous wave swept us both away. I could not swim, but I was lucid. I knew that a storm was coming.

The next day I decided to build an ark like Noah in the Bible, except in the form of a pimped out yacht. Russell Crowe volunteered to captain the vessel. He had a vision of the apocalypse as well, but his involved virus-ridden toads falling from the sky and infecting the human race. His advice was, "Smile, we might be dead by tomorrow." From on the whale-infested water, there wasn't much sign of a storm.

It was hard to keep the animals from killing each other. I watched a gorilla fight a leopard. The gorilla won, but his upper body was torn to shreds. Russell Crowe got scared and abandoned ship. Since I assumed it was going to rain, I had not brought any water on board to drink. I drank from the sea monkey tank while trying desperately not to drink the sea monkeys. My guilty conscience was getting the better of me. My conscience was similar to the simians that controlled the whales from the inside. Their brains connected through the cerebellum.

I realized that the simians were using the whales as filters, and protection from harm. Then I realized that I was using the pimped out yacht for the same reason. Then I realized that I was a simian, and began to cry softly. The exquisitely simple surface of the ark, the mouth of the whale, a vast, vulnerable space where I could see the horizon in every direction, was open to an endless amount of feelings that were every bit as complex and unfathomable as the ocean itself. I stood there, wondering which way was home. There was no way to know.

When Nature Calls

I was standing on the edge of a cliff with Jim Carrey, observing as an army of killer bees invaded an eroded Los Angeles landscape. The killer bees swarmed the San Fernando Valley, threatening to sting the population to death for turning their backs on nature. I kept telling Jim Carrey to be aware of the cliff's edge, but he was hypnotized by the black and yellow collaging between the buildings. I was worried that he would plummet to his death, leaving me alone at the top.

Jim Carrey told me that I was mistaken to be afraid of the plunge and that the descent would be glorious if he did go over the edge. It would be the greatest feeling in the world to fall, exhilarating beyond comprehension. It was the collision with the ground that was cause for worry. He said to beware of smashing my body against the rocks below and that seeing the end before I reached it was the most important thing.

At the top of the cliff where we stood, there was an oak tree that was rumored to have been there for thousands of years. Some people said that when the tree was just a sprout, the first pyramids were still being built as tombs for the pharaohs. It was guarded by an enormous electric fence until the California exodus occurred, and people in their frantic state tore the fence down, shocking themselves as they tried to escape the killer bees. I climbed the oak tree to get a better look over the valley and to get shade from the sun that was burning the back of Jim Carrey's neck.

I ran my fingers through the leaves and felt a cool breeze blow through the branches. I was distracted and didn't notice Jim Carrey inching imperceptibly forward. Then I heard it, his scream of joy as he fell from the cliff. I called his named and ran to the edge, crawling when I got close and looked down. Then I saw it: Jim Carrey was flying.

He flew through the air like an eagle, smiling as he flapped his arms. He flew along the ground, then up again, looking at me the entire time with both his thumbs up to indicate his excitement. He flew without watching where he was going, and into a swarm of killer bees that were just waiting to sink their stingers into the flesh of a human. I couldn't bear to watch, but I listened as the laughs transition into screams. It was too much for me to handle.

The Sky Is Crying Every Day

I was reading a book about the occult when a smiling Bjork interrupted me. She wanted us to get dressed in human butterfly costumes and fly around the town at night looking for quiet places to sit and hum. I said that I wished we could fly to Neptune, and Bjork nodded in agreement. Then she told me to get my wings on so that we could get going.

Bjork and I fluttered through the clouds, flapping our arms in a motion that suggested not only flight but also kindness and sincerity. There was the sound of flutes playing in the distance, the sound of harps, and gravel rattling. Bjork landed next to a quarry and sang, "Imagine what my body would sound like slamming against those rocks." I imagined that it would sound beautiful, like a whisper. The night would heave like a deep breath before all was silent again.

We flew over an airport to watch planes take off. Most people had a desire to launch downward into space where they could grow like fungus in the dark. Bjork and I had other aspirations, but we had taken the time to read nature as a parable. Nature wasn't nature until just recently. It was magic only a day ago, in the sorcerer's cauldron, stirring like a dragon in a dungeon. It was there before we knew what it was. There were things that science couldn't save us from, like when my wisdom tooth shattered on a popcorn kernel or the time Bjork was a victim of dark magic by a jealous critic who cowardly pushed pins into a voodoo doll instead of facing Bjork with courage.

Jet exhaust lay in a depressing collection of rainbows. The chrome left polychrome scrapes across the asphalt. It was raining, and the colors ran together like wet sidewalk chalk. The scene was too sad to stare at, and I flew away. I thought Bjork would follow me, but she stayed behind to watch the puddles of color move and dance. I felt like the universe was rearranging itself while my heart broke. It was the true essence of nature, and there was nothing anyone could do to escape it.

"Nothing is so wretched or foolish as to anticipate misfortunes. What madness is it to be expecting evil before it comes."

— Lucius Annaeus Seneca

The Smell of Death is Everywhere

There was a dog park in my neighborhood marked by an inexplicable statue of a soft pretzel in the center. The park was between two churches where locals often walked with their pups to meet other pet owners and play fetch. There were large signs warning people not to climb the trees, and to pick up their dog's poop. I had a pet schnauzer that would pee in excitement whenever he saw the soft pretzel statue.

I met many hot, young couples at the dog park, but the one who I remembered meeting the most was Khloe Kardashian and Lamar Odom, who together had a boxer puppy named Bernard Hopkins. I first spotted Bernard Hopkins between two rustling bushes and asked him where his parents were.

An elderly man was reading the newspaper on a camping chair nearby. At first, I thought that the pungent stench of the elderly man was overwhelming. Then I realized he was sitting by his dog's grave, and felt remorse for judging him so hastily. I asked him if he knew where Bernard Hopkin's people were, and he pointed me in the direction of Khloe Kardashian and Lamar Odom, who were following their natural inclinations to dig for lizards in the dust.

I approached them and introduced myself as the groundskeeper of the dog park. My biggest job was to watch out for groundhogs, which had the habit of trying to fight dogs for trespassing on their territory. The ground was loose beneath me, and I could tell that a groundhog's burrow used to be there. Khloe Kardashian said that Bernard Hopkins was trained for search and rescue should any dogs be injured in a groundhog fight. Lamar Odom kept sneezing due to his pollen allergy, and the row of sunflowers that I haphazardly kicked when I first approached them.

My knees were filthy, and my wool socks were patchy and torn. I felt embarrassed due to Khloe Kardashian's pink latex dress, and Lamar Odom's expensive gray sweatshirt, which made me look like a forager in comparison. They both kept asking about the terrible smell coming from the subterranean soup that was the elderly man's dead dog, and I told them that it must have been coming from a nearby factory. Bernard

backpack, and then took off into the night. She licked my hands as I ran. Maybe nobody deserved Bonny, but she couldn't survive by herself, in the wild. There were wolves in those woods. I'd seen them when I was a boy and remembered how their yellow eyes looked under the full moon. If I set Bonny free, she would be eaten by morning.

When my yard came into view, I noticed the red lights of a police car in the distance. I crawled with Molly on my back and peered over the picket fence. My neighbor's house had cops swarming all around. Some were taking pictures, some smoking cigarettes. A few took pictures with the chickens. I heard the muffled crying of my neighbors.
Then the officer said, "I don't write the zoning codes, I just enforce them. The dogs can stay."

"What about my Bonny," my neighbors replied. "You have to find her. We're owed that much."

"We have our best men on it, ma'am." said the officer. Then I heard the sound of panting and Bonny's barks behind me. I turned around to see a wolf, its yellow eyes staring directly at me. A head poked over the fence, one of the police officers.

"Captain, come quickly! I've spotted the dognapper!" said one of the cops. "Look, there's a wolf!" I cried, pointing at the darkness. "Jesus, kid," the officer replied. "Could you be any more cliché?"

I shared my cell with a man that had no eyebrows. He was a tall man, with hairy skin and a plaid shirt. He scowled at me crossly. This man clearly did not like being put in a box. He was not used to boxes. My father eventually bailed me out. He didn't speak to me until we reached our driveway.

"Why did you do it?" he asked me. "It was just a misunderstanding," I said. He shook his head, stepped out of the car, and said, "Well, Spock is going to be sleeping in my bedroom from now on. I just can't trust you near him." Then he went into the house.

Spock was my dad's Boston terrier and the most annoying dog on the planet. He was prone to walk across my crotch every time I watched television and twice peed on my bed. Both times my father blamed me. I waited a few minutes before going inside, lighting the butt of one of my dad's leftover cigarettes that was sitting in the ashtray. It tasted like shit. It felt like freedom.

As I stepped out of the car, I heard Bonny's barks. She was following a firefly that led her to my feet. I bent over to pet her, but the firefly skipped back through the air, and once again the chase was on. I looked up and saw my neighbors standing there. She gave me a glare of pure malice. He gave me the middle finger. "Right back at you," I told them and kept on walking until I reached the house and closed the door behind me.

Can I Get a Witness

I sat in the interrogation room at the end of the hall. The LAPD arrested me, specifically Jackie Chan and Chris Tucker. If it were up to me, I would have just told them the person responsible for the string of dognapping's so that I could go home and maybe get there before dinner. But I knew snitching was not an option. The kids at school made that very clear. They told me that snitches got stitches. My father once said that too.

"Tell us again," said Jackie Chan. "I need to make sure that we have everything straight. You were not at Lucy Liu's birthday party on the night her dog went missing?" I said nothing. "Why don't you tell us the reason you were in her backyard that night," urged Chris Tucker.

I shrugged. "Don't be nervous," said Jackie Chan threateningly. I tried to speak up, but it came out in coughs. "Was this your first time stealing someone's pet?" Chris Tucker asked. "Have there been others?"

"No, I didn't steal anything," I said. Jackie Chan smirked at me. "Well, I guess we got our facts mixed up." He looked at Chris Tucker. "I suppose if there's nothing else you'd like to tell us that you can go."

I stood up. "I need to finish my homework," I mumbled. "Well we need some answers out of you," said a frustrated Chris Tucker. He sighed a long sigh. I let my hair fall over my eyes so that it was hard to tell if they were open or closed. I pulled my curls back so that the police officers could see that I wasn't crying. They whispered to each other, then left the room.

A minute later they opened the door and sat back down. "We just got off of the phone with Lucy Liu," Jackie Chan said. "She's willing to drop all of the charges if you tell us where her dog is, and apologize in person."

I said nothing. As the police officers waited for my response, I thought about how upset my parents were going to be no matter what happened. Chris Tucker repeated Lucy Liu's proposition. I said, "This is harassment, and I refuse to say anything more without a lawyer present."

Startled, Jackie Chan and Chris Tucker both leaned back in their chairs.

They looked at me with newfound respect. "Am I free to go?" I asked. "You're excused, but don't leave town," said Jackie Chan. I paused for a second, and then said, "I live in my parent's basement. Where would I go?"

Sinister Purposes Are Not Always Public

I needed money to buy beer for the weekend and decided to answer an advertisement on Craigslist for a lucrative babysitting gig. The ad stated: *Playful Primate Needs A Nurse For The Night.* The monkey in need of supervision was named Jonah Hill. Jonah Hill was Russell Brand's pet.

Russell Brand gave me a bottle of pills, which he said were prescribed by a veterinarian for Jonah Hill, with a label that read, *Side effects may include: sleepiness, or unusual drowsiness, trouble sleeping, bloated or full feeling, crawling, itching, numbness, prickling pins and needles, or tingling feeling, chills, cough, decreased appetite, excess air or gas in the stomach or intestines, fever, constipation, decreased interest in sexual intercourse, diarrhea, dry mouth, ejaculation delay, heartburn, inability to keep or have an erection, loss in sexual ability, desire, drive, or performance, general feeling of discomfort or illness, increased sweating, joint pain, muscle aches and pains, not able to have an orgasm, pain in the neck or shoulders, headache, increased thirst, muscle pain or cramps, nausea or vomiting, shortness of breath, swelling of the face, ankles, or hands, unusual tiredness or weakness, pain or tenderness around the eyes and cheekbones, runny nose, shivering, sneezing, sore throat, stuffy nose, tightness of the chest, tooth problems, unusual dreams, unusual drowsiness, dull tiredness, weakness, or feelings of sluggishness, yawning, coma, confusion, convulsions, decreased urine output, dizziness, and fast or irregular heartbeat.*

Seeing the look of terror on my face, Russell Brand told me that, before adopting him, Jonah Hill had been trained in the arts of villainy and arson, the latter of which had become his hobby. Medication kept the monkey on an even-keel and helped with his horrific stomachaches.

When Russell Brand left for the Red Carpet, I flushed the pills down the toilet, and instead of dosing Jonah Hill, decided to read him a bedtime story, which put him right to sleep. I too was feeling a bit tired and decided to take a nap next to him.

When I awoke, the sheets, the bed, the book, the room, and everything else in the house was all on fire. I ran all over the place looking for Jonah

Hill, trying to make monkey noises that he might recognize, but could not find him anywhere. When Russell Brand returned and saw his house ablaze, he seemed surprisingly calm. I told him that Jonah Hill must have thrown up the pills before they digested, due to his horrific stomachaches.

Russell Brand agreed that this was a logical conclusion to draw, and could not prove otherwise because his house, and all of his possessions, except Jonah Hill, who I had eventually found trying to strike a match next to a neighbor's propane tank, were in ashes on the ground.

Establishments That Confine Animals Are Inherently Evil

My phone started to ring while Jeff Goldblum and I dug up dinosaur fossils in the middle of the desert. The phone call was from Kellogg's who claimed that Jeff Goldblum and I won a sweepstakes trip to their private island. Jeff Goldblum did not want to take a break from our excavation but agreed when they said that, in addition to the private island getaway, our entire trip would be paid for, including food and travel expenses.

On the plane, Jeff Goldblum talked my ear off about chaos theory and said that eventually all islands would be underwater. Kellogg's private island was a submarine volcanic mountain covered in fog. Jeff Goldblum screamed, "Look at all of those gorgeous women!" pointing to a series of female velociraptors roaming beneath us. When I saw the dinosaurs, I immediately began to feel nauseous. I had just ingested mushrooms so that I would be tripping before we landed, but felt incredibly overwhelmed now that I knew we would be on the same landmass as prehistoric predators. Jeff Goldblum reassured me that the private island would be totally safe, even though he had little to no knowledge about it.

When we landed, we were given a tour of the surrounding beaches. There were electric fences all around, so we couldn't touch the sand. At all times, we were protected by armed guards that gave the private island a highly militarized atmosphere that did not help my trip. Jeff Goldblum was drunk and didn't care that we were in an unsafe environment where the armed guards executed the inhabitants if they acted out.

That night there was a terrible storm. A bolt of lightning struck one of the electric fences, creating a gap in the dirt where the dinosaurs could crawl through. Jeff Goldblum woke me up and told me that there was something I had to see. I looked outside, rubbing the window with my sleeve so that I could see better. All around us, there were velociraptors having sex in the pouring rain. According to Jeff Goldblum, it was a breeding ceremony due to high levels of horniness and adrenaline.

When they finished having sex, the velociraptors were hungry, and looking for meat to eat. We were the closest food and knew that they would be able to break into our bunker with ease if we didn't get help soon. Luckily,

Jeff Goldblum has a cousin in the National Guard, who was crazy enough to believe our story and sent a helicopter to pick us up. The helicopter sent the velociraptors into a frenzy, running back toward the beaches as fast as their tiny legs could move. Jeff Goldblum and I just stood and waited until the aircraft was low enough for them to drop a ladder, which we climbed to safety as they transported us off of the island.

We were put in a three-star hotel and politely asked to sign waivers saying that we would not sue. Since nobody was injured during the trip, Jeff Goldblum and I were pretty indifferent to the experience and stated that we would not sue on the condition that Kellogg's put our picture on the cover of their newest cereal. Cold cereal was Jeff Goldblum's favorite food, so I let him pick the name. The newest cereal was called, "Goldblum Grahams," which were little, crisped squares made of whole wheat and sugar. It tasted pretty bland, but Jeff Goldblum loved them, so I smiled instead of suing.

"Hunger, prolonged, is temporary madness! The brain is at work without its required food, and the most fantastic notions fill the mind. Hitherto I had never known what hunger really meant. I was likely to understand it now."

—Jules Verne

Mayonnaise Malaise (The Solution Is Sushi)

Tom Hanks, who once had the clean-cut charm of a choirboy, scraped toast as a callous misanthrope, arguing with customers at length for no apparent reason. He wore the same three-piece suit to work each day, overdressing to compensate for a lack of showering. Some days his smell was so bad that it overpowered the sandwiches and customers who came with an appetite left with nothing.

Still, there was a light in Tom Hanks' eyes that shined in spite of the dark circles beneath them, like moons eclipsing themselves. Maybe he hid his happiness inside where only he could experience it. Or maybe he was a ghost of his former self. Or maybe he was drunk. Maybe he was a drunken ghost who was damned to sell sandwiches solemnly for eternity.

One day when school let out, I followed the other kids across the street to get something to eat. I still remember how Tom Hanks' eyes stopped shining as he saw us approach. He looked like he just saw a ghost, or like he just saw his reflection for the first time in a long time. My hungry classmates stormed his stall with the force of a thousand winds, shaking and shoving their money in his face, as they demanded sustenance.

Tom Hanks stood back, overwhelmed, unsure what to do. In the end, he did nothing. He abandoned his stall and watched as we all tore it apart with the understanding that he couldn't stop us if he tried. This was the moment that Tom Hanks' retired from the sandwich business. He was ready to see what else the world had to offer. Specifically, he wanted to give sushi a try. Maybe, he thought, sushi would bring him back to life.

Romanticizing the Wasted Time of My Youth

I used to work with Sarah Silverman in the dining hall of an old folks' home. She handled the register while I scooped porridge for the residents. The porridge was gray and clammy. I remember one day, looking around the kitchen and realizing that the porridge was all that there was to eat. A Band-Aid from one of the residents may or may not have fallen into the porridge that morning. I was desperately hungry, but knew that the porridge could have been from a few days before; new porridge was swapped in to serve on an irregular basis.

Sarah Silverman begged me, "Please do not eat the porridge," and then said, "You might die." She told me that the residents were already dying and that she did not want to see the same happen to me. That was when I realized that the porridge was what was keeping the residents old. It was not providing them with the nutrients that they needed to survive.

I decided to crush up a bottle of multivitamins, and a half-ounce of marijuana to mix in with the porridge. After lunch, the residents seemed much more healthy and much more stoned. An old man, who appeared around thirty to forty years younger following mealtime, approached Sarah Silverman and said that his testosterone was finally balanced enough to ask her out on a date. Sarah Silverman said, "I am so flattered," several times in a row without ever actually giving a firm "Yes," or "No," in response to the old man asking her out on a date.

An old woman, who also appeared thirty to forty years younger, approached me and asked if I could sell her any weed. I told her that she should use the money she had saved to find a new place to live, maybe in Colorado so that she could buy weed legally. She said that she was poor, and looked sadly into the porridge chafer, which for the first time in months was empty. I could tell that she had a comprehensive longing—for a lover or a friend, for a past time or place, for a different version of herself. She wanted to relive the frantic, neurotic joy that came with being a child.

Sarah Silverman offered to let the old woman live in her guest house in California, to which the old woman replied, "You are my savior," and proceeded to dance. I told Sarah Silverman that what she had done was very kind, as did all of the other residents, who at that point were gathered around us asking, "Do you have any other spare guest houses?" Since Sarah Silverman had done a good deed, I wanted to help too and offered to be the nursing home's on-call drug dealer. The residents screamed, "Hooray," and I rolled up my other half-ounce in celebratory joints to keep the elderly people young and happy until I could re-up.

The World Is a Cesspool but My Heart Tells Me to Hold on Just a Little Longer

One scorching summer day, I decided it would be fun to build a lemonade stand. Hilary Duff helped me hand-squeeze nearly a thousand lemons in preparation. There was pulp all over the place. Hilary Duff saved the seeds. She told me that when she was a little girl, there was the most wonderful lemon tree in her backyard, which she used to climb with her sister. Then Hilary Duff said that she was going to plant a seed on the lawn outside of her apartment complex where a tree could grow, so that whenever she looked out of her window, she could stare at it for a while, and remember those old times.

I set up the lemonade stand, which was just a table, on the side of the road, which was a four-way intersection. It was a high traffic area for cars and customers alike. Our first customer was a man on a motorcycle. He pulled up the little window on his helmet and poured the lemonade through the hole without us ever seeing his mouth. Then he threw a dollar down before zipping around the corner.

A car coming through the intersection almost hit the man on the motorcycle and beeped for approximately ten seconds before pulling over on the side of the road to calm down. The driver was a high school football player according to his oversized purple football jersey that said Roman Catholic High School across the front. He asked us, "Did either of you see that asshole?" I said, "We sold that guy lemonade right before you pulled up."

The high school football player looked at me with an expression somewhere between disgust and intense dehydration. I could tell that he did not want to support a stand that would sell lemonade to an asshole like the man on the motorcycle, but that he was also very thirsty. Hilary Duff offered him a two-for-one deal, and then gave me a look as if to ask, "Is it okay that I just did that?" I nodded, and she nodded too, reassured.

After taking a sip from his first cup, the high school football player spit all over the front of the stand saying, "This is the worst batch of lemonade I have ever tasted!" That was when I realized that the high school football player was probably the type of person who preferred Gatorade or other artificial sports drinks to quality, hand-squeezed beverages. Hilary Duff shook her head, realizing that she had indeed made the wrong decision by offering a two-for-one deal to a guy who turned out to be a bigger asshole than the man on the motorcycle.

It was an awkward moment for both of us, and I considered taking down the stand if we were only going to get assholes, but just then a minivan pulled up. Several children, each in soccer cleats and kneepads, ran out screaming "Lemonade!" A man with curly hair, and a polo shirt that said "Coach" followed them out, and yelled, "One cup per person!" I offered them the pitcher, and said, "This one is free." I looked to Hilary Duff for reassurance, and she gave me two thumbs up. I gave her two thumbs up, reassured. The curly-haired coach said, "Alright guys, but only two cups maximum. I do not want any of you sugar-crashing halfway through the game."

Then one of the children said, "This is the best lemonade I have ever tasted!" Hilary Duff nodded her head, realizing that we had finally found the right clientele. We kept the stand open for the rest of the day, and only got one more asshole. The rest of the customers were dog walkers and cyclists.

Eye Widening Terror Caused by Contemptuous Behavior and an Alarming Shade of Pale

There was an old banana stand near the beach that burned to the ground before being rebuilt as a fast food restaurant and purchased by Jason Bateman. Apparently Jason Bateman's plan was to blackmail his old associate Michael Cera into managing a restaurant for him. He said that he would do everything in his power to make Michael Cera's job a living hell, but wouldn't say why.

For example, I was on my way to work one day and stopped in to grab a breakfast sandwich. When I went to order, I saw Jason Bateman holding Michael Cera's head over the deep-frier, and asking him, "What have we always said is the most important thing?" Michael Cera kept responding, "Family," when the answer Jason Bateman was looking for was, "Breakfast."

There were no other human employees at the fast food restaurant; the crew was made up entirely of artificial intelligence. Each robot waiter had the same name, "Salty," and would say a quick hello before its touch screen chest expanded for the customers to place their orders. Jason Bateman kept joking that Michael Cera and Salty were his slaves and programmed them to call him Master. "But Master Bateman," Michael Cera interjected before being slapped with a cold dishtowel across the face.

I was worried for Michael Cera's safety and decided to call the Department of Labor to investigate Jason Bateman's operation. The first thing that the Department of Labor found was that the breakfast sandwiches contained trans fat and pigeon meat.

Michael Cera claimed that he knew nothing about the ingredients used for making the food, but he was the one who handled the deliveries when they arrived and made all of the meals, so it was confusing. When I pressed him, Michael Cera changed his story and said that Jason Bateman threatened to beat him with a broom handle if he disobeyed. I pressed him even further, and he stated that by "broom handle," he meant, "box cutter," and by "beat," he meant "murder."

The Department of Labor sent out their top investigator, Ice-T, to see if he could figure out what was wrong with Jason Bateman. After only five minutes, Ice-T determined that Jason Bateman was "wack," and "refusing to keep it real." Every time Ice-T asked Jason Bateman a question, Jason Bateman would pretend to be hard of hearing, and Ice-T would respond, "Are you going to make me smack you?" Eventually, after a long and arduous questioning, Jason Bateman confessed to his part in the fast food restaurant's illegal ingredients and abuse of Michael Cera. It would have been more satisfying if he hadn't cried so much during his confession, but a win was still a win.

I thanked Ice-T for taking the time out of his day to help me out, and he nodded approvingly. He looked over at a horny Michael Cera, who was pretending to flirt with one of the Salty robots, then at Jason Bateman, who was breathing hot air against the window of Ice-T's police cruiser, and trying to spell out the word "Sorry" with his nose on the glass. Ice-T just shook his head and said, "I will never understand white people," before driving off.

Embracing Life's Misinterpretations

It was only four degrees, and everybody at the train station looked chilly, including Aziz Ansari, who was impishly jumping back and forth in his oversized goose down parka, trying to keep warm. I asked if he knew what time the train was coming. He said, "It will get here when it gets here," which I thought was a nice sentiment, but at the same time I needed to get downtown where I worked part-time as a barista at Starbucks.

I had missed the prior three days of work with a sore throat, which was tender from smoking abnormal quantities of marijuana while I Skyped with my Internet pen pals. One pen pal was from Istanbul, and the other was from Connecticut. Aziz Ansari said that he was born in Columbia, South Carolina, which he was embarrassed to tell people because of the racist and homophobic sentiments associated with South Carolina. He said that in addition to these assumptions, the city of Columbia was also home to the Secession Convention that enabled South Carolina as the first state to depart from the Union leading up to the Civil War. I said, "That is a real bummer."

It was a very brief moment, but that only made my restatement all the more devastating. "That is a real bummer, bro." It was becoming increasingly unclear whether I was offering some awkward form of sympathy or a tactless insult to injury.

When the train came, Aziz Ansari walked with his head down into quiet ride car, where he could be alone with his thoughts. My only thought was whether I would be able to walk, or if I would have to run to make it to Starbucks by the start of my shift. My boss said that I was a good employee, always opening on time, never late. The only reason I had missed the last three days of work was because it was the last week of my two-week notice, and I just wanted to be done already.

The next time I saw Aziz Ansari, which was just a few minutes after running ahead of him off the train, he was standing in line waiting for a Peppermint Mocha Frappuccino. I wanted to apologize for my lack of etiquette in our earlier conversation but wondered if that would only make things worse.

When I called his name, Aziz Ansari approached and paid without a word. He walked with his head down like Charlie Brown, with the dull, trudging commitment that came with being an outlier. His isolated existence lurched forward at speeds both too fast and too slow, but when he took that first sip of his Peppermint Mocha Frappuccino; it was like everything in his life had fallen into place.

Munchies Hijack the Hypothalamus and Spawn an Undeniable Impulse to Feast

It was a beautiful day on the pot farm. Ex-presidents were tilling the soil, and police officers monitored the plants to make sure no pests disrupted the process. Whoopi Goldberg and Woody Harrelson were my chaperones. They took me on an exclusive tour, showing me everything from the sun-grown sprouts to the 100% custom-mixed on-site soil. Whoopi Goldberg said that all of their marijuana was spring-watered, slow-cured and hand trimmed by volunteers.

"Shamanic fasting pro-tip," Woody Harrelson interjected, "Inhale massive quantities of marijuana smoke to accelerate your fast into deeper levels through the day while suppressing hunger." I was confused. Marijuana smoke always made me hungrier. Then Whoopi Goldberg said, "Our marijuana causes you to become so euphoric and creatively inclined that you don't have time to feel hungry."

I wanted to try it, so I smoked a joint of their best strain, which they called "Whoopty Doo" because it was as close to a combination of their names as they could make. After a few puffs of Whoopty Doo, I felt nothing. Then, out of nowhere, a phoenix soared down from the heavens and snatched an anteater off of the ground while performing a barrel roll maneuver. At least, that's what I thought I saw. I was super high.

The next thing I knew, I was sitting in the backseat of my Honda Civic scooping melted gelato from a waffle bowl with my dirty hands. My entire existence leading up to that point played through my mind like a movie – from my modest start as a child actor on PBS to my spectacular rise to soap opera stardom, the booze and constant partying, and predictable spiral out of control.

On my journey, I'd realized that human attention could be magical when turned toward a particular symbol. Mine was the pot leaf. An occultist introduced me to chaos magic and showed me how sigils such as the pot leaf could gain potency when you focused on them. From a mental standpoint, it was as if I was hacking my brain to propel myself toward the specific goal of getting high. I was able to take the idea of being stoned and distil it down to its most condensed and freebase form. Eventually, I was able to become high just by staring at a pot leaf for a few minutes.

With that said, my tolerance was not ready for Whoopty Doo, and when Whoopi Goldberg and Woody Harrelson found me, I was upside down, licking lint off of the carpet with my eyes shut. It took me a while to remember what happened, but when I did it was quite embarrassing. Whoopi Goldberg and Woody Harrelson were cool about it and gave me an ounce of Whoopty Doo in case I ever wanted to try it again. I did as on my way home and ended up in a Burger King drive-through. I couldn't say the result was much different.

"A person needs a little madness, or else they never dare cut the rope and be free."

— Nikos Kazantzakis

I Have Tried to Live an Honest Life, but It Has Given Me Nothing Back but Emptiness

Aubrey Plaza stabbed me in the arm with a fork after I told her that there was no such thing as the tooth fairy. She twisted the prongs and called me a liar. Aubrey Plaza did not lose any of her baby teeth until she was thirty years old. She thought that her mouth was a gold mine, with an appreciating value that grew as she did. Aubrey Plaza lost her first tooth when I playfully smacked her in the face with a pool noodle at the YMCA. One lost tooth formed a trend. The next day she lost another, then another, until her mouth was completely toothless.

That evening I told Aubrey Plaza that the tooth fairy was not real. In retrospect, the arm forking was a fair reaction. After all, I had hit her pretty hard in the face with that pool noodle. Before going to sleep, Aubrey Plaza told me that she was going to put the teeth under her pillow, despite my lies. I wanted to pay for her teeth, but I was poor and unemployed. All I had was a five-dollar bill, which I was able to sneak under Aubrey Plaza's pillow before she woke up.

The next morning she showed me the money, and said, "I told you so, liar." I smiled with enough strain that Aubrey Plaza realized that I was not really smiling, but only attempting to smile for her benefit. She asked me why I was not genuinely happy to hear that the tooth fairy existed. I told her I was euphoric and tried to appear less like I was trying to smile, which only made me look even more like I was trying to smile. Aubrey Plaza called my face "annoying," and playfully smacked me in the cheek with a frying pan, which minutes before I had used to cook her favorite food, bacon, just in case she was still upset with me.

I stumbled forward and hit my head on the kitchen counter. Unconscious, I fell face-first onto the floor, my mouth striking against the ground, which knocked my two front teeth loose. They were adult teeth. Aubrey Plaza smiled and said, "Look, we are matching!" The physical and emotional toll that followed was more than enough to make me reconsider my beliefs regarding the fantasy figures of my childhood.

I wanted to take a time machine back to before I told Aubrey Plaza that there was no such thing as the tooth fairy, but it was too late. The damage was done, and while her childlike certainty in the supernatural somehow endured, my face was left with a gaping hole. I wanted so badly to believe in magic, in a mystic pixie that hauled around bags of teeth, a worthless commodity, yet somehow maintained a never ending cash flow.

I was merely too encumbered by an accumulation of blasé disappointment, which started when I was five, the day I lost my first tooth, and everybody in kindergarten said I looked weird and called me a "toothless freak." I hoped that I could at least get some money out of the situation, but when I woke the following morning to check under my pillow, I found nothing except a note that said, "You get what you get, and you don't get upset," attached to a can of tuna.

Our pantry had more cans of tuna than any other in the Tri-County. None of us even liked tuna; mom just bought it because it was cheap. At first, I thought that the tooth fairy might have made a mistake, and accidentally thought that because there was so much tuna in the house, that I must enjoy it. Then I thought about the note, and nothing made sense.

I went downstairs and showed my mom, who was eating a can of tuna for breakfast while she paid her bills. She replied, "Brush your teeth," with breath that smelled like tuna. I looked at one of the bills on the table and saw that my mom's handwriting looked exactly like the handwriting on the note, confirming that the tuna was indeed not from the tooth fairy, but from my mom.

I asked her, "Why? Why did you give me a can of tuna instead of money?" She responded by holding up one of the invoices to my face. "You see this?" she asked pointing to the bill. "This costs money." Then she pointed at me. "You cost money too. So until you have a job, and start paying some rent, you better get used to disappointment," she wiped her mouth, "and the taste of tuna."

Some Things Sting Before They Warm (Lightning is like a Shot of Tequila)

Splashing in puddles made me feel like I was being born, or baptized, or something. Blake Lively said that storms made her feel lively. We both thought that the rain felt good until it got cold, then we felt like the rain might make us sick. There was a tree breaking apart in the wind, which Blake Lively called "the snake tree," by the way its branches looked like serpents hissing at the sky.

I told her that standing under trees during thunderstorms was dangerous because of lightning strikes, and then realized that I probably sounded like a paranoid old man, like maybe my father, who had conservative tendencies despite referring to himself as left-wing.

Blake Lively said, "It would be cool to see a lightning strike," then looked away distractedly. I offered her a cigarette, and she declined, saying she did not smoke, though it was tempting because smoking in the rain seemed like a sort of a romantic thing to do.

She told me it was getting late, and that she should probably get a move on if she was going to catch the bus, even though a bus came every ten to fifteen minutes depending on traffic, which was light on rainy days. I told her to be careful, and when she asked, "Why?" I said, "Lightning Strikes."

The World Is Filled with Too Many Restless People in Need of Rest

I was having trouble with insomnia and desperately needed a sleep aid. First, I tried melatonin. That gave me waking nightmares, so I tried listening to Jeff Bridges' Sleeping Tapes instead. I closed my eyes and pretended that Jeff Bridges and I were going for a walk like two old friends on a Sunday. It was profoundly soothing and filled with intriguing sounds and noises that gave me a very pleasant overall listening experience. My problem was that the imagery Jeff Bridges painted with his words was too vivid for my mind to handle, so I still couldn't fall asleep.

Next, I tried listening to a Tiger Woods narrated version of The Jungle Book. That was tranquilizing at first, but just as I was about to fall asleep Tiger Woods interrupted me. Apparently he confused himself with the tiger in the story. He had gotten particularly mad at the passage that read, "He heard the dry, angry, snarly, singsong whine of a tiger that has caught nothing and did not care if all the jungle knows it." In response, Tiger Woods went on a ten-minute rant regarding his narration, claiming that he did not have a "dry, angry, snarly, singsong whine," but more of a "deep, syrupy, sexy, rich, baritone voice." To me, he sounded painfully insecure.

Finally, after being up for a week straight, I called my friend Adele to come over. Adele was a pretty good singer and agreed to croon me to sleep if I babysat her cat while she was on tour. I was allergic to cats, but at that point, my desperation for sleep outweighed the risk of my throat closing up and killing me. Adele sang me a song called Daydreamer that caused me to fall asleep at exactly three thirty-three in the afternoon. It was as if her lullaby had cast a spell on me, causing me to slumber for a week to make up for the time I'd spent awake.

Unfortunately, I didn't realize this would happen. I had work the next day and missed my shift at Starbucks. My boss fired me via text message, which was the first thing that I saw when I woke up. It didn't matter, though. I felt refreshed and ready to take on the world, and not even a multinational corporation like Starbucks could stop me.

Short Term Disappointment

I was walking down the highway in New Jersey with a hundred dollars in my pocket when Val Kilmer pulled over to give me a ride. He said that he'd take me as far as New Mexico on the condition that I accompanied him to see his sister's production of Hamlet first. When we arrived at the theater, Val Kilmer said that he did not have any cash on him, and I had to pay for both of us, which amounted to a hundred dollars. He was wearing short shorts, flip-flops, and a dress shirt that was far too large. I was wearing jeans and a hooded sweatshirt.

We sat in the front row of the balcony, in front of an old woman who said I looked like a thug, and that Val Kilmer looked like a mistake. The play was running thirty minutes behind schedule, and Val Kilmer became so bored that he started firing spitballs at the folks seated below.

The people were furious. They ordered that Val Kilmer exit the theater, but he refused. He pulled a paintball gun out from beneath his oversized dress shirt and began firing wildly around the theater. The old woman behind us called him a terrorist. I told Val Kilmer that the old lady was right, that he was a mistake. The audience tried to escape as paintballs flew and splattered green and blue all over the red felt carpet, and red velvet curtains.

I decided to pretend like I didn't know Val Kilmer, that despite paying for his ticket, and sitting next to him, we were in no way associated. Val Kilmer realized I did not support his paintballing by the way that I turned away from him and looked at my phone as if oblivious to the chaos going on around me.

He shot the phone from my hand with surprising accuracy. I was sure that the paint had ruined it, which meant that Val Kilmer had cost me hundreds of dollars by that point. When I left the theater to look for a payphone to call my parents, Val Kilmer chased after me, saying he was sorry, and that he would pay for the phone. He wrote a check that said, "Pay to the order of a million dollars," with the memo, "Just kidding. You aren't my friend anymore." I told him that we were never friends. I didn't make friends with people who I met on the road. From my experience, those relationships only led to heartbreak and regret.

Getting Used to Public Humiliation

I was grumping around an elementary school playground during recess, and the children were ignoring me. I kept telling them to slow down. Since none of them acknowledged my existence, I assumed that I must have been invisible. Since I was invisible, I decided to do whatever I wanted. I pushed a child off of the swing set, even though there were plenty of open swings next to him.

An audience of parents gathered around me, so I assumed that I was not invisible anymore. I decided that, since I had their attention, I might as well give them a show. I got some serious height on the swing and executed a perfect front flip through the air, landing like a cat on all fours. Everyone applauded.

Robert De Niro stepped out of the crowd wearing a Hawaiian shirt and a monocle. He said that the elementary school playground was actually the set of his new movie, "The Adventures of Rocky and Bullwinkle 2." I'd wondered why there was a moose tied up with a squirrel saddled to its back. Robert De Niro said that the children and audience of parents were actually movie extras and that he was impressed by how my display of aerial movement inspired them. As a reward, he told me I could share his lunch.

Robert De Niro's lunch was a steak. The steak was raw. There was no chef on the set, no assistants, and I realized that Robert De Niro expected me to be the one who cooked his steak. I had little experience barbecuing, but agreed to try. While the steak was cooking, I talked to Robert De Niro about his life. He didn't have much to say. In fact, he was stuck after, "Life is good." Still, I was hypnotized by his presence and lost track of time as the steak continued to cook.

Once the steak began to burn, Robert De Niro finally spoke. He said, "What are you doing? Don't overcook it, bring it over!" When I did, he looked down at his plate with a super hungry, super disappointed expression. He looked a bit like a basset hound, but less cute. I wanted to die. I knew I had failed him. I had failed myself. I made a terrible first impression. Robert De Niro would always remember me as the guy who intruded on the set of his movie and ruined his lunch. Then I thought about how hard it was to get any information out of Robert De Niro concerning his life, and how most of his days were probably just a blur anyway. It was the first time that I felt good being forgotten.

"Too much sanity may be madness and the maddest of all, to see life as it is and not as it should be."

— Miguel de Cervantes

Life Has the Potential to be Validating and Enriching

Jesse Eisenberg pointed across the bar and told me to watch. I did not seriously think that he was capable of drinking ten shots in ten minutes, but he proved me wrong. He said that getting drunk was all about the pre-drinking meal, which for him was spaghetti and bread, and for me was nothing. I felt sick after my third oatmeal stout. My conundrum was always whether to drink the low carbohydrate beer with the low alcohol content or drink the high carbohydrate beer with the high alcohol content? In the end, it always worked out the same, with my head spinning, and my stomach feeling queasy.

Jesse Eisenberg became thoroughly drunk within approximately an hour to an hour and a half after drinking ten shots. I would have described his attitude at that time as "sassy." Jesse Eisenberg got "sassy" when he snapped his fingers at the bartender in a misguided attempt to get his attention. In return, the bartender ignored Jesse Eisenberg for approximately twenty minutes. Since I associated with Jesse Eisenberg, I too was ignored for approximately twenty minutes. I sulked until the bartender looked at Jesse Eisenberg and asked, "Are you ready now, your majesty?"

Jesse Eisenberg, who disregarded the bartenders remark regarding his royal status replied, "Yes, three shots of tequila for my friend here," gesturing towards me, which, combined with the DJ's choice to play Protect Your Neck by the Wu-Tang Clan, put me back into a great mood. I yelled, "Drinks all around!" Everybody in the bar cheered. Then a thought came to me, that I could use my money for something better than buying booze for strangers, like donating to a homeless shelter. I announced, "I changed my mind, no drinks." Everybody in the bar booed, even when I tried to explain that the money was going to the less fortunate. I asked Jesse Eisenberg if he wanted to tag along to the homeless shelter and he said, "Right now?" I could tell that his heart was not in it, even after he said, "Sure, why the hell not?"

When we arrived at the homeless shelter, there were plenty of people around. It was cold out, and many of them had no place else to go. I asked one of the men if he knew where I should bring my donation. He said, "Right here," then called me a "poser," and accused me of trying to purge my white guilt with cash, rather than compassion. I looked over my shoulder to see Jesse Eisenberg darting in the opposite direction. I told the man that he had a fair point, and that maybe I was not truly as empathetic as I pretended to be, and certainly not as charitable, but that I was trying to do better.

Then I gave him all of the money in my pocket and told him not to spend it all in one place. The man said that he did not have many friends left, and asked if I wanted to shoot pool with him. I told him that I would play next time I came around, which I promised would be soon.

As I walked away, back toward the bar, my head began to spin in a way that turned my world upside down, causing me to become motion sick, and to vomit oatmeal stout and three shots of tequila all over my white button-down shirt. The man laughed until his legs gave out, breathless, turning blue. He said, "That's just what I needed, a laugh. I guess you are good for something." I smiled, despite the fact that I received the white button-down shirt as a birthday present from my father, who I hardly ever saw because he lived on the west coast. I smiled despite the fact that I told my father, "This is the greatest shirt I have ever owned," the moment I saw the shirt because it was from him, and nobody else. When the man stood up from laughing, he reached to give me the shirt off of his own back. He held it out and said, "This is the least I can do."

I put the man's shirt over my shoulders like a blanket that came down to my knees. I thanked him with my whole heart, and said, "This is the greatest shirt I have ever owned." I held out my hand for a shake, and the man held out his knuckles for a fist-bump, pointing to the vomit on the ground and saying, "Germs." I nodded, and said, "I feel you."

You've Got to Pick a Pocket or Two

I was going out with Anthony Bourdain to get a bite to eat and maybe a drink or two. We were going to a restaurant called The Olive Garden because Anthony Bourdain had a coupon. We took an Uber and passed through a trendy area with lots of places to get drunk. There were the ritzy clubs with cover charges over twenty dollars, the college watering holes, the post-college hangouts, the rave warehouses, the sports bars, the upscale taverns where politicians, lobbyists, and lawyers all gathered to get bent. We were planning on bar hopping when our stomachs were full.

The Olive Garden was a large, dimly lit dining room. It was empty, and we pretty much had our choice of seating. There were candles on every place setting that appeared quasi-romantic. Only one table was taken by what appeared to be a therapist with two separate families, both white trash, but from different parts of the United States. One family was clearly from the south while the other seemed like they were from the midwest. It was a boisterous group, and they were banging on the seats of their wrap-around booth as they squabbled.

For some reason, Anthony Bourdain wanted to take the table right next to theirs, but I suggested the one that was ten feet away. At first, it was hard to understand their accents, but once we got attuned Anthony Bourdain and I could overhear every word of the white trash families' conversation. They were talking about the baby that the two youngest at the table had out of wedlock, and who was financially responsible.

The therapist's voice sounded super familiar, and I tried to figure out where I had heard him before. Anthony Bourdain recognized it too and told me that the voice belonged to the former Democratic mayor of Cincinnati, Jerry Springer.

Jerry Springer was trying to mediate, but he was in over his head. Both families were threatening his life, and he just kept nodding his head, agreeing with each side like a good politician. When the waitress came out, she put a bill in front of Jerry Springer, who claimed he had no cash or credit card on him. Both families started screaming at Jerry Springer, as did the waitress who demanded her money.

175

Anthony Bourdain intervened, and despite not wanting to spend money on an expensive meal, offered to pay for all nine of the people sitting with Jerry Springer. The former Democratic mayor of Cincinnati thanked us, and left in a hurry with his white trash clients, none of whom wanted any part in purchasing the food that they had just consumed.

Anthony Bourdain smiled at me and flipped open the billfold in his hand so that I could see the license on the inside. The license belonged to Jerry Springer. I was confused. Anthony Bourdain explained that he was a master pickpocket, having developed his skills back when he was a cocaine addict and needed money to score. He showed me that Jerry Springer had five hundred dollars cash in his wallet.

I was shocked that Jerry Springer would try to dine and dash like that, but I guess I underestimated him. I underestimated Anthony Bourdain as well, thinking he'd developed a conscience when really he was a master thief and a culinary vigilante. I even underestimated The Olive Garden's cuisine, which turned out to be scrumptious. I had pasta in sauce topped with chicken and cheese with salad and breadsticks. Anthony Bourdain decided to get drunk instead of eating. He said it would save him money, and make him feel better about himself. I didn't object.

A Moment of Ugliness Alternated with Beauty

I was hosting a book release party for my friend Molly Ringwald. Everybody was in good spirits, and most were on drugs. All was going according to plan until I entered the line at the buffet and noticed something disturbing. The caviar was missing. I'd laid out the dishes myself only ten minutes before and did not understand how a group of people could eat an entire platter of fish eggs so quickly. Then I noticed Channing Tatum, and saw that he had taken the liberty of removing the caviar from the buffet, and onto his lap, where he was cramming it into his mouth by the spoonful. I asked, "Is that not the rudest thing?" to nobody in particular.

Channing Tatum and I made eye contact from across the room, and I tried to appear noticeably perturbed by his selfish display. Channing Tatum raised one eyebrow as if to ask, "Are you leering at me?" I responded by nodding vigorously. Channing Tatum still did not understand the implication and continued to shovel caviar into his mouth. His cheeks became so full that fish eggs were falling from his lips like little raindrops that splattered against his khakis. A sad-faced Robert Pattinson approached, his baleful eyes appearing like cups of coffee as he asked me where the caviar was. I pointed towards Channing Tatum, who was holding his stomach and saying, "I do not feel so good." Robert Pattinson said, "Serves you right!"

I helped Channing Tatum to the bathroom, where he threw up everything he had just eaten. The caviar fell from his lips like little fishes returning to the water where they belonged. He kept saying, "Sorry, not sorry," and, "It was fun while it lasted." I told Channing Tatum that he was not allowed to eat anything else, and for the first time, he appeared genuinely embarrassed. That was when I noticed how truly handsome Channing Tatum was, aside from the snot hanging from his nose. He said, "Sorry, bro." When he called me "bro," I smiled for what felt like a very long time.

Sentimentality Elicits Sympathy (A Bruised Angel's Transition from Being a Child to Being an Adult)

Sarah McLachlan's parents went sailing for an entire summer, leaving her in a cottage in Nova Scotia with their friends, a couple of marine biologists and three Labrador Retrievers that never stopped barking. "Don't they keep you up at night?" I asked, seeing the dark circles beneath her eyes. "My walls are pretty thick," she said. She mumbled something else. Her lips were thin and puckered. Everything else about her looked tired.

"They kill animals and bring them to my door. Last week they tore apart a fox," she said, digging through her grandpa's sock drawer to find rolling papers. At fifteen, Sarah McLachlan already had a taste for the finer things. She kissed a joint together with the precision of a veteran stoner, smoking so that she could forget all of those dead animals.

"Where are your mom and dad now?" I asked. Both of our parents coincidentally had boats offshore of a posh marina in Antigonish. We had a mutual aversion to the sea. "Montreal," she declared, in a flippant, highfalutin voice.

We snuck into the kitchen for munchies when the Labrador Retrievers went outside. We searched every cupboard before finding an unlabeled box underneath the sink, obscured by a sheet of dirt. I hoped we would find a plankton net or an extravagant bong. Instead, there was a jigsaw puzzle. I grinned at it, realizing we now had a summer project, split into a thousand tiles.

One afternoon, with nearly five hundred pieces fully interlocked, Sarah McLachlan said I was smarter than her. I didn't know what to say because she was the most intelligent person I knew. She'd constructed most of the panoramic landscape by herself while I got high and frivolously tried to help.

"What do you want to be when you grow up?" she asked. "An archaeologist, but I'm not totally sure," I said. Sarah McLachlan took a hit from her homemade apple pipe, then looked at me with eyes that were stale and dim. "My parents are never coming back," she said.

She explained that her parents were moving to Montreal and that she was to stay with the marine biologists and their Labrador Retrievers. That way she wouldn't have to get used to living somewhere new halfway through secondary school. They wouldn't live together as a family, but they would send her letters.

The week before summer ended we finished the puzzle—a beautiful portrait of the Valley of the Ten Peaks. Tracing my hand across Moraine Lake, I admired its dazzling blue. There was one space at the crest of Mount Little. I gave the tile to Sarah McLachlan. She took my hand, and we pressed the piece down together. Then I saw it on her face. She was all grown up.

Ignorance is Bliss

I was on the beach in Miami when I saw a blinding light. The sky was gray, it was a misty day, and I had no idea what the source of the light was. It was a reflection coming from Matthew McConaughey's compact magnifying mirror. He was staring at his reflection sensually and clearly wanted to have sex with himself. It was an unbridled display of vanity, him standing there in his leather chest girdle and hot pants, gyrating his hips back and forth, thrusting as men and women walked by him. It didn't seem like he was trying to seduce anyone, more that he had an infatuation with himself that provoked him to show off his dance moves.

Matthew McConaughey's true hedonism surfaced when he took off his pants. He was wearing a leather thong underneath and began doing backbends, asking people to spot him so that he didn't contuse his spine. Then he took his shirt off and wore nothing but a knapsack and a bandana while he did pushups. Tourists started taking pictures of him, and whenever a camera flashed Matthew McConaughey would approach it like a shark tasting blood.

I approached Matthew McConaughey when he was in the middle of doing burpees and offered him a few puffs of my marijuana cigarette. Matthew McConaughey responded, "I smoked the weed Castro smoked in the mountains before he took over," pointing across the Atlantic Ocean at where he thought Cuba was. He was pointing toward The Bahamas.

When I asked him if he wanted to go swimming, Matthew McConaughey insisted that the ocean was too cold to live in, and compared it to a Russian strip club with no heat. It was not a joke, but he kept laughing about it. He laughed so hard that he started to cough, and then to choke. The lifeguard ran off of his stand to give Matthew McConaughey CPR, but it was no use. He'd found his own joke so hilarious that he couldn't stop smiling as he gasped for air.

Everyone around thought that he was just kidding, and clapped their hands and laughed as the lifeguard bashed Matthew McConaughey's chest with his fists like an ape. Eventually, Matthew McConaughey was able to calm himself down, but not before his torso turned completely black and blue from the beating that the lifeguard gave him. The rest of his body was sunburnt and red as a lobster. I was unsure how he was able to take so much punishment while still putting on a show and genuinely laughing until I saw Matthew McConaughey walk back to his beach bag and pull a bagful of MDMA out of his towel, which he proceeded to snort directly off of in front of everyone. He literally did not care. Matthew McConaughey explained that, regardless of the stakes, his body would always be shredded, which was what mattered to him the most in the world. Then he told me that he was thirsty, and went running toward the ocean to take a drink.

A Complete Surrender to Natural Impulses without Restraint or Moderation

One beautiful morning, I took a trip to the beach with Uma Thurman and John Travolta. John Travolta was wearing a pair of Bermuda shorts and applied a generous amount of zinc oxide to his nose while Uma Thurman carried the umbrella and towels to a sunny spot on the sand. I was more than a bit uncomfortable in my denim jeans and flannel shirt.

Upon reaching the oceanfront, John Travolta took out his arm floaties and blow-up duck inner tube, secured them to his body, and sprinted into the water, releasing a shriek of unrequited glee as a wave came crashing down on his head. I raced after him and dove under the surf, laughing as I popped my head up to see that we had inadvertently scared several children with our frolicking. Uma Thurman was back on the beach, busily tanning her pastel-colored skin.

Much to the chagrin of the lifeguard, John Travolta began to dunk me mercilessly. The families around us gasped. The children began to cry, and their parents prayed that John Travolta would cease dunking me before it was too late. Seeing that I was starting to lose consciousness, Uma Thurman stopped lying still to run over, with a leash, which she wrapped around the neck of a giddy John Travolta, pulling him to shore while she repeated, "Somebody needs a timeout."

I gasped for breath and watched John Travolta gag as his body dragged across wet sand. The lifeguard warned Uma Thurman that if John Travolta misbehaved again, he would have to leave the beach. Even though the lifeguard was wearing sunglasses, I could tell that he was very serious. John Travolta looked like a wax figure of himself, melting under the sun.

Uma Thurman said that whenever John Travolta got out of control, hyperactive, or on cocaine (that day he was all three, unbeknownst to me), that the best thing to do was let him swim it off. Uma Thurman and I sat in the sun and watched the crash and foam of waves crashing and breaking against the shore as John Travolta swam laps toward the horizon, only raising his head to breathe, and scream "You will never catch me, now!"

Eternal Rest

I dreamt that there was a shadow creeping around the back of my beach house, on a golden carpet made of sand, which pulled vertically any three-dimensional object that crossed its path, be it the weight of a crab or a pillar. The stalker made of shade luckily weighed less than nothing. That was the summer, the same summer that I thrust a spike through the skull of a living dead lurker.

In my sleep-deprived state of delirium, I decided to name the zombie Beautiful Existence. I threw Beautiful Existence into quicksand and watched him sink. A figure in the distance was Jude Law. Jude Law kept dying and returning to life like the other zombies. Then I realized that the beach house was actually haunted, filled with the ghosts and incarnate corpses of former vacationists.

I went inside of the beach house to explore. The architecture was freakishly bizarre. There was a reptilian creature, bone-white and sallow, creeping out of a pit in the basement. His grinding jaw and square eyes sketched me out. He was the Grim Reaper. His breath smelled like death.

I was relying on my contingency plans for time travel to facilitate my escape when I punched the Grim Reaper in the face, knocking loose one of his teeth. I thrust the enormous incisor through the head of a zombie that I mistook for Jude Law, who I thought had come back from the dead to kill me. I decided to name the second zombie Paisley.

Paisley did not die right away. He managed to grab me by the throat with his teeth. Then I saw a flash of light and was suddenly in another place and another time. It was much colder there, but the snow on the ground was melting. A sign read 'Purgatory,' but that made no sense to me. Although neither did the zombie apocalypse, at first, and everybody adapted to that. All I wanted was to see Beautiful Existence one last time. I owed an apology to both him and Paisley, for misjudging their appearance, and not accepting them for what they were: dead.

Printed in Great
Britain
by Amazon

32114081R00111